FRIENDS OF ACPL

Carleton Renaissance Plays in Translation

General Editors: Donald Beecher, Massimo Ciavolella

Editorial Advisors: H. Peter Clive, Gordon J. Wood, J. Douglas Campbell, Leonard G. Sbrocchi, Mark Phillips

Carleton Renaissance Plays in Translation offer the student, scholar, and general reader a selection of sixteenth-century masterpieces in modern English translations, most of them for the first time. The texts have been chosen for their intrinsic merits and for their importance in the history of the development of the theatre. Each volume contains a critical and interpretive introduction intended to increase the enjoyment and understanding of the text. Reading notes illuminate particular references, allusions, and topical details. The comedies chosen as the first texts have fast-moving plots filled with intrigues. The characters, though cast in the stock patterns of the genre, are witty and amusing portraits reflecting Renaissance social customs and pretensions. Not only are these plays among the most celebrated of their own epoch, but they directly influenced the development of comic opera and theatre throughout Europe in subsequent centuries.

In print:

Odet de Turnèbe, **Satisfaction All Around (Les Contens)**
Translated with an Introduction and Notes by Donald Beecher

Annibal Caro, **The Scruffy Scoundrels** (Gli Straccioni)
Translated with an Introduction and Notes by Massimo
Ciavolella and Donald Beecher

Giovan Maria Cecchi, **The Owl** (L'Assiuolo)
Translated with an Introduction and Notes by Konrad
Eisenbichler

Jean de La Taille, **The Rivals** (Les Corrivaus)
Translated with an Introduction and Notes by H.P. Clive

In preparation:

Lope de Vega y Carpio, **The King and the Farmer** (El Villano
en su Rincón)
Translated with an Introduction and Notes by Adolfo Lozano
and Michael Thompson

Alessandro Piccolomini, **Alessandro**
Translated with an Introduction and Notes by Rita
Belladonna

Jacques Grévin, **Taken by Surprise** (Les Esbahis)
Translated with an Introduction and Notes by Leanore
Lieblein and Russell McGillivray

Carleton Renaissance Plays in Translation

Jean de la Taille

THE RIVALS

(Les Corrivaus)

Translated with an Introduction and Notes by
H.P. Clive

Wilfrid Laurier University Press

1981

Canadian Cataloguing in Publication Data

La Taille, Jean de, 1533-1611 or 1612
  The Rivals

(Carleton Renaissance plays in translation,
ISSN 0704-4569 ; 4)
A play
Translation of: Les corrivaus.
Bibliography: p. xxx-xxxii
ISBN 0-88920-120-X

I. Title. II. Series

PQ1628,L35A6413 1981   842'.3   C81-094501-0

Copyright © 1981, Carleton University Renaissance Centre &
Wilfrid Laurier University Press
Waterloo, Ontario, Canada N2L 3C5

80 81 82 3 2 1

Typeset by Carleton University Graphic Services

2233699

Acknowledgements

I am grateful to my colleagues Albert Halsall and Mark Phillips for their valuable comments on an early draft of the introduction and translation. I owe a special debt to Donald Beecher who proposed many improvements in the tone and balance of the dialogue. My wife advised, with her usual patience and acumen, on numerous problems of vocabulary and style. Last but not least, I should like to thank my daughter Vanessa for her careful examination of a later draft; she will recognize many of her suggestions in the final version.

H.P.C.

Ottawa,
August 1980.

Introduction

Renaissance comedy

Les Corrivaus is one of the most attractive examples of the new type of comedy developed in France during the second half of the sixteenth century. The principal dramatic genres popular in the Middle Ages — mystery plays, moralities, and farces — for which the humanists expressed such haughty disdain (cf. the Prologue to our play), gave way to tragedies and comedies inspired by the classical tradition. The ancient models for the comedy of the Renaissance were the plays of Plautus (254-184 B.C.) and Terence (195 or 185 - 159 B.C.), whilst the most important source of classical theories on the drama was the grammarian Aelius Donatus (mid-4th century A.D.). In addition to composing a treatise on tragedy and comedy (*De tragoedia et comoedia*), Donatus wrote commentaries on five of the six comedies of Terence. Both the treatise and the commentaries were printed in numerous editions of Terence's plays throughout the sixteenth century.[1]

At the same time, French humanist comedy came to be increasingly influenced by the Italian learned comedy (*commedia erudita*) which was itself modeled on the same classical authors. Among the most famous Italian writers of such comedies were Alamanni (1495-1556), Aretino (1492-1556), Ariosto (1474-1533), Bruno (1548-1600), Dovizi, called 'Il Bibbiena' (1470-1520), and Machiavelli (1469-1527). Several of their plays became known in France, at first through the editions published in Italy[2] or some French translations (cf. Section iv below), as well as through occasional performances, such as those of Bibbiena's *La Calandria*[3] at Lyons in 1548 and of Alamanni's *Flora* at Fontainebleau in 1555. Later in the century, the establishment of Italian troupes of actors in France offered the educated public greater opportunities for acquainting itself with the Italian plays.

The neo-classical comedy consists of five acts which, as a rule, are preceded by a prologue. The acts are usually divided into a number of scenes, to mark the entrance and exit of the characters. The most distinctive feature of these comedies is, of course, their happy endings, and most of them conclude with one or several marriages. The plots are splendidly romantic and full of sentimental attachments, dramatic complications, perils, abductions, mistaken identities, and recognition scenes. Stock characters abound, such as old men in love, pedantic scholars, parasites, braggart soldiers, gluttonous lackeys, and procuresses. But despite the conventional nature of these various types, the authors frequently manage to endow their characters with distinct personalities.

Unlike classical and neo-classical tragedy which depicts the awesome experiences, often based on historical or pseudo-historical incidents, of persons of exalted rank and position, Roman and Renaissance comedy presents a fictitious story dealing with the lives of ordinary folk and their servants. La Taille alludes to this aspect in the Prologue to *Les Corrivaus*, which also echoes the oft-quoted remark attributed by Donatus to Cicero, that comedy is an imitation of life, a mirror of manners, and an image of truth. Such a definition clearly implies that, like tragedy, comedy is capable of serving a moral purpose: it can provide instruction as well as entertainment. 'A comedy', writes Donatus, 'is a play . . .

in which it may be learned what is useful in life and what, on the other hand, is to be avoided.'[4] La Taille produces the desired edifying effect in his comedy by presenting and discussing such favourite themes as the often reprehensible behaviour of young people and the responsibilities of parents towards their children, especially as far as the arrangement of suitable marriages is concerned. What is more, he achieves this didactic purpose of comedy without the usual extensive moralizing and constant recourse to proverbs and maxims. As a result, *Les Corrivaus* is likely to appeal more strongly to the modern reader than some other comedies of the period.

Les Corrivaus

i Author

Jean de La Taille was the older son of Louis de La Taille, seigneur de Bondaroy, whose domain was situated in the Gâtinais region to the south of Paris. Jean was born in 1533 or shortly thereafter, and is believed to have died in late 1611 or in 1612. After attending the Collège de Boncourt in Paris from about 1550 until 1556, he read law at Orléans. He seems, however, to have felt little enthusiasm for his legal studies, for he soon returned to the capital where he occupied his time increasingly with literary pursuits.

La Taille fought in two of the early wars of religion: during the first (1562-1563) he served in the Catholic army, but in the third (1568-1570) he joined the Protestant forces. His biographers, most of whom regard him as a Huguenot either by birth or at any rate of long standing, have found it difficult to account satisfactorily for his divided loyalties. Perhaps D.L. Drysdall is right in suggesting that the La Taille family was not converted to the new faith until the late 1560s.[5] This could explain Jean's absence from the second war (1567-1568) and his change of allegiance in the third. At the end of this latter war, during which he was wounded, Jean retired to Bondaroy where he was to reside for the remainder of his life.

Jean de La Taille is best known for his four plays, all of them probably written not later than 1562, and for the short treatise *De l'art de la tragédie*, which was composed, or at any rate revised, at a later date and was printed as a preface to *Saül le furieux*, the more famous of his two neo-classical tragedies on biblical subjects (the other was *La Famine, ou les Gabeonites*). His two comedies were *Le Negromant* [*The Necromancer*], a prose translation of Ariosto's *Il Negromante*,[6] and *Les Corrivaus*, which is generally regarded as the earliest original prose comedy written in French during the Renaissance. The four plays were first published in the two-volume edition of La Taille's works which appeared in Paris in 1572-1573. Some of La Taille's later poems were included in the *Parnasse des poètes françoys modernes* published in 1578. His last work is believed to have been the *Discours notable des duels* (Paris, 1607).

ii   Editions

The earliest known edition of *Les Corrivaus* is that contained in the second volume of La Taille's collected works published in 1572-1573 (Paris: Fédéric Morel). This collection was reprinted in 1598 (Paris: Fédéric Morel) and again in 1602 (Paris: Robert Fouët). In modern times, the play has been edited by René de Maulde (in *Oeuvres de Jean de La Taille*, Paris: Willem, 4 vols, 1878-1882, reprinted Geneva: Slatkine, 2 vols, 1968); by Kathleen M. Hall and C.N. Smith (in *Jean de La Taille: Dramatic Works*, London: Athlone Press of the University of London, 1972); by Giuseppe Macrì ('*Les Corrivaus*': *Commedia del Rinascimento francese*, Galatina: Editrice Salentina, 1974); and by Denis L. Drysdall ('*Les Corrivaus*': *Édition critique*, Paris: Didier, Société des Textes Français Modernes, 1974).

iii   Date

The early editions of *Les Corrivaus* give no indication of the date of its composition. The approximate date can, however, be deduced with a fair measure of probability from internal and external evidence.

In the play (IV.v), Fleurdelys is said to have been five years old when her father abandoned her during his flight from Metz, an event which can be assumed to have occurred in April 1552, since it was in that month that the French troops entered the city (see Section vii below). Elsewhere in the play (II.i), Fleurdelys is described by Euvertre as now being a beautiful girl of fifteen, which would place the action in or close to 1562.

The *editio princeps* of *Les Corrivaus* contains a prefatory sonnet by Jacques de La Taille, the author's younger brother. Jacques is known to have succumbed to the plague in April 1562. His sonnet was evidently intended to introduce the play in an edition which must therefore have been planned at the very latest during the early months of the year 1562 (the long delay in publication could well be due, at least in part, to Jean de La Taille's participation in the wars of religion).

If one assumes, as seems plausible, that *Les Corrivaus* was already finished by the time Jacques wrote his sonnet, the *terminus ad quem* of its composition is obviously April 1562. As for the *terminus a quo*, the internal evidence set out in the second paragraph of this section suggests that it should not be placed more than a few months earlier. It thus appears reasonable to conclude that the play was written either late in 1561 or in the first months of 1562.

iv   Sources

The principal source would appear to be tale V.v of Boccaccio's *Decameron*, the summary of which can be translated as follows: 'Guidotto da Cremona entrusts his young daughter to Giacomo da Pavia and dies. Giannole di Severino and Minghino di Mingole fall in love with her in Faenza and fight over her. The girl is discovered to be Giannole's sister and is given in marriage to Minghino.'

Boccaccio's story contains most of the essential elements of La Taille's plot, in particular the rivalry between two young men who are in love with the same girl; their determination, in the face of parental opposition to the match, to possess the girl by whatever means should prove the most expedient; the help provided by the servant and the chambermaid; the lovers' almost simultaneous attempts to seize the girl; their fight and subsequent imprisonment; the recognition of the girl by her real father, thanks to a distinctive mark under her left ear; the consequent identification of one of the young men as her brother; her betrothal to the other one, and the release of all the persons arrested during the quarrel.

The presence of so many important identical features in the Italian story and in the French play leaves little doubt of La Taille's considerable indebtedness to Boccaccio. More specifically, there are strong indications that he relied heavily on Antoine Le Maçon's French translation of the *Decameron* (Paris, 1545), for both the play and the summary given of its plot in the Prologue present striking textual similarities with Le Maçon's version.[7]

In addition, La Taille drew to a significant extent, both textually and in other respects, on the following two Italian comedies: *I suppositi* [*The Pretenders*][8] by Ariosto (1509) and *Gl'ingannati* [*The Deceived*], a collective work by the Accademici Intronati of Siena (1531).[9] From internal evidence, it seems very likely that La Taille once again used French translations: for *I suppositi*, probably that published by Jean-Pierre des Mesmes under the title *Comédie des supposez* (Paris, 1552);[10] and for *Gl'ingannati*, Charles Estienne's version, originally entitled *Comédie du sacrifice* (Lyons, 1543) and later renamed *Les Abusez* (Paris, 1548, 1549, 1566).[11]

Some other models have been tentatively proposed, notably the comedies *I due felici rivali* [*The Two Fortunate Rivals*] by Jacopo Nardi (1513) and *Il viluppo* [*The Imbroglio*] by Girolamo Parabosco (1547). But D.L. Drysdall, who discusses the question of sources at some length in his edition of *Les Corrivaus*, maintains that these two Italian comedies differ in so many significant details from the French play that it is highly unlikely, despite the striking similarities in the plots, that La Taille used them as sources.[12]

Lastly, *Les Corrivaus* clearly bears the general imprint of Roman comedy. In addition, H.W. Lawton has shown that in several scenes La Taille drew on particular passages of Terence's plays.[13]

v   Prologue

The Prologue consists of two parts, of which the second presents a partial summary of the plot. The first part contains a fierce attack on the mediaeval comic theatre, coupled with a strong plea for its replacement by the type of comedy which *Les Corrivaus* is said to represent — a comedy inspired by classical and contemporary Italian models.

While it is not known whether La Taille had any personal contacts with members of the Pléiade group of writers — he may very well have made their acquaintance during the years he spent in Paris — he evidently shared whole-heartedly their desire to create a new French literature based on the classical tradition. Like Du Bellay in the *Deffence et illustration de la langue françoyse* (1549), La Taille calls for a break with the immediate past and for a return to the literary ideals of the ancients; and like Du Bellay, he links his invitation to French writers to equal the achievements of the ancients with a bold affirmation of the excellence of the French language.

vi   Plot

At the same time as he streamlined the main subject of Boccaccio's story by discarding some aspects which were of only marginal interest to the rivalry of the two lovers, La Taille enriched the plot by adding the character of Restitue and a subplot of which she is the centre. Restitue is a typical 'protatic' character, that is to say one who is introduced at the outset of a play but is not used again during the rest of it (the 'protasis' is defined by Donatus as 'the first act of the [comedy], in which part of the plot is unfolded, part concealed for the purpose of holding the audience's expectation'[14]). The function of such a protatic character is thus to develop the exposition, and this role Restitue fulfils most effectively and with great economy. From her conversation with the Nurse, with which the play opens, we learn that she is pregnant; that the man responsible for her pregnancy is Filadelfe; that he has abandoned her to pay court to Fleurdelys; that Fleurdelys is also loved by Euvertre; and that she prefers Euvertre to Filadelfe. We further gather that Filadelfe's father is expected to join his son in Paris in the near future — in this way the author prepares us for Benard's arrival in Act IV. At the same time, the first scene also starts the action of the play with the hatching of the plot for Restitue's removal to the country. This apparently ingenious solution of her dilemma will lead to the summoning of the doctor and, as a result of his visit, to the discovery of her pregnancy by Jacqueline. Incidentally, Restitue makes a silent re-appearance in the final scene of the play, as does the similarly protatic Polinesta — on whom Restitue has most probably been based — in Ariosto's *I suppositi*.

The efficient use which La Taille makes of Restitue as an instrument of exposition enables him to conform quite easily to Horace's precept that the action of a play should begin *in medias res*, in the middle of the plot. In this way the spectator's interest is focused from the outset on the most dramatic event which results from the incidents related in the exposition. The plot of *Les Corrivaus* clearly reaches its climax in the lovers' attempts to seize Fleurdelys. The action of the play is accordingly set on the day when these attempts are to be made. The timeliness of Benard's arrival on that very same day is merely one of those extraordinary coincidences so commonly found in Renaissance comedy. La Taille, far from underplaying its improbability, seeks rather uneasily to account for it by making one of the servants express his wonderment at the mysterious ways of Fortune (IV.i). This 'explanation', incidentally, was also taken over by La Taille from Ariosto's *I suppositi*.

As well as serving an expository function, the presence of Restitue produces a more balanced, though perhaps a more contrived, ending than the one offered by Boccaccio. In the *Decameron* Giannole, once his consanguinity with Agnesa has been established, is largely left out of the happy conclusion to the story; not so Filadelfe, for whom a prospective bride is waiting in the person of Restitue. La Taille's determination to leave no loose ends even prompts him to arrange the marriage of Benard and Jacqueline, a fate which they accept with the equanimity traditionally displayed by characters in learned comedy who find themselves unexpectedly thrust into holy matrimony at the end of a play. This triple marriage, piling up improbability on unlikelihood, as it does, shows what an exceptionally high degree of conventionality a Renaissance audience was prepared to accept.

vii   Historical note

It is explained in IV.v that Fleurdelys was abandoned by her father and found by Fremin during the hours which respectively preceded and followed the occupation of Metz by the royal army. A brief account of the historical background may therefore be of interest.

By a treaty signed at Lochau in October 1551 and subsequently confirmed at Chambord in January 1552, King Henry II of France concluded an alliance with the German Protestant princes against the Emperor Charles V. The agreement provided for the King to take possession of those cities which, although they belonged to the Empire, were not German-speaking. The most prominent were Metz, Toul, and Verdun, all three of them situated in Lorraine. To the French, this agreement offered a welcome opportunity to consolidate and extend the country's north-eastern frontiers.

A large French army was quickly raised for the purpose of marching to the Rhine. The bulk of the forces was sent on ahead into Lorraine under the command of the High Constable, the Duke of Montmorency, leaving Henry himself to follow at a more leisurely pace. Montmorency soon occupied Metz (in April 1552) by a mixture of intimidation and guile. As Benard indicates, the arrival in the vicinity of so large a royal army threw the inhabitants of Metz into a panic. Montmorency had therefore little difficulty in obtaining acceptance for his proposal that, while his army of almost 40,000 men would camp outside the city, he and his staff should be quartered inside. He then moved in, not with a few attendants as had been expected, but with 1,500 select troops. After that, any resistance would have been useless. Thus Montmorency took possession of Metz without opposition by what amounted to a confidence trick. The unexpectedly rapid and bloodless manner in which it was seized by the French accounts for Benard's remark that he would not have fled if he had known that the city would fall in the way it did.

viii Time-sequence

There is no reason to think that the period covered by the action exceeds the length of the performance. Since no mention is made of any time having elapsed between the different acts, the play can be produced with a complete continuity of action, as is the case with the comedies of Plautus and Terence.

The action begins in the latter part of the day. At the end of the opening scene, the Nurse remarks that Filadelfe has not been in the house 'to-day' ('aujourd'hui'), thus implying that the major part of the day is already over (in order to make the meaning quite clear, 'to-day' has been replaced by 'all day' in the translation). A little later Filadelfe tells Claude that he sent his lackey out three hours earlier to look for him (I.v). And elsewhere both Euvertre (II.i) and Alizon (II.ii) refer to 'this morning' in a way which plainly indicates that they are now speaking in the second half of the day.

Once the action has started, little time is lost: Claude promises Filadelfe that he will be able to enter Fremin's house within the hour (I.iii), and Alizon likewise assures Euvertre that Fremin will be setting out for the town very shortly (II.ii). Claude's explanation to Alizon in III.iii that he is holding a torch because he is about to fetch his master home suggests that dusk cannot be very far away. Lastly, Felix's complaint about not having eaten supper yet (IV.iii) also fits in well with the general conclusion that La Taille has placed the action of his comedy in the late afternoon or early evening.

ix Decor and staging

The fact that nothing is known about any sixteenth-century performances of Les Corrivaus should not be regarded as in any way reflecting on the stageability of the play, for records of theatrical performances during the Renaissance are extremely rare. It is clear that a production of Les Corrivaus would have posed no problems whatsoever in terms of contemporary theatrical practice.

The stage set for a Renaissance comedy normally

presents a neutral space — for instance a street, as in our play — surrounded on three sides by representations of houses or other buildings. In a book published in Paris in 1545, Sebastiano Serlio (1475-1554), the influential Italian architect who spent the last thirteen years of his life in France, proposed a comedy decor consisting of seven buildings: a church at the back, two houses and an inn on the left of the neutral space, and three houses on the right (Serlio's model is reproduced on the cover of this volume).

In actual fact, all that is needed for a performance of *Les Corrivaus* is a street, with two 'compartments' representing the houses of Jacqueline and Fremin. A third house may be assumed to belong to Calixte (see II.i), but none of the stage action takes place in it. Filandre's house, which is said to be close by (V.v), could also conceivably be visible on the stage.

The audience can observe all the movement in the street, and all the comings and goings through the front doors of Jacqueline's and Fremin's houses. On the other hand, as a glance at Serlio's model will show (and his decor is typical in this respect), the spectators watching a Renaissance comedy normally had no view of the backs of the houses occupying the stage. Consequently, in the particular case of *Les Corrivaus*, they would not have seen the back door of Fremin's house, through which the lovers and their companions enter. Filandre and his guard evidently also approach the house from the rear, since the audience is unaware of their arrival until informed of it by Felippes (III.vi). That the fighting likewise takes place out of sight of the spectators can be fairly satisfactorily justified by the circumstances of the plot: Filadelfe enters the house, seizes Fleurdelys, her shouts bring Alizon to her aid and their combined screams are heard by Euvertre who rushes in and grapples with Filadelfe in an effort to free Fleurdelys — which makes it logical that the fight should at least begin inside the house. Some of the ensuing free-for-all must, however, spill over into the space behind the house, for the scandalized neighbours are hardly likely to give expression to their anger by hurling stones and torches *into* Fremin's house! This would also explain why Filandre straightaway makes for the back of the house. For the same reason, Gillet fleeing from the 'battlefield' and Felippes escaping from Filandre's men probably do not run out through the front door, but appear from the side of the house, having fought or been arrested behind it.

La Taille, then, has managed to arrange his plot in such a way that it provides adequate reasons for the fighting to take place where the audience cannot see it. In so doing, he has conformed to one of the principal conventions of the neo-classical theatre, which decrees that violent actions should not be shown, but described — a rule which offered especially to writers of tragedies numerous opportunities to display their rhetorical skill and verbal brilliance (among the most celebrated 'purple passages' in French drama are the spine-chilling accounts of tortures and executions in Garnier's *Les Juifves* (1583) and, a century later, the 'récit de Théramène' in Racine's *Phèdre*).

To return to the matter of the decor: one consequence of the audience's inability to see the backs of the houses is that the quarrel between the two servants — one of the most amusing scenes of *Les Corrivaus* — has had to be placed in front of the house. This is not very plausible in terms of the plot. Since Claude and Alizon have arranged to give their signals from the back door, one might expect them to get ready to do so *behind* the house. As it is, when Claude moves off at the end of the quarrel, one must presumably imagine that he then dashes round to the rear of the building in order to wave his torch, out of sight of the audience, to the waiting Filadelfe (III.iii). A more careful author might, of course, have solved this particular problem of plot construction

more convincingly. But Renaissance audiences were no
doubt far less troubled by such logical inconsistencies
than present-day theatre-goers are likely to be.

The entire play, then, takes place in the residential
street in Paris which constitutes the 'neutral space' of
the decor — with the possible exception of the opening
scene which, as K.M. Hall and C.N. Smith have suggested in their edition of *Les Corrivaus*,[15] was perhaps
meant to be performed in a loggia forming part of
Jacqueline's house. The first house on the right hand
side in Serlio's decor (see cover) offers excellent examples of the two types of loggia represented on the Renaissance stage: the arcade (or entrance porch) at street-
level, and the open-air room situated above it. Normally,
however, such representation would have been "flat"
and not three dimensional. Of course, some modern spectators might be surprised that such a confidential talk
should be held in an open space at all, whether it be a
street or possibly a loggia, rather than inside the house;
but La Taille was simply following contemporary theatrical practice, under which the entire action of a learned
comedy normally took place out of doors. He evidently
did not think it necessary, therefore, to justify a situation which, after all, would not have unduly puzzled
audiences familiar with the conventions of Italianate
comedy. It is, however, interesting to find that Ariosto,
at the beginning of the century, had made a point of
offering an explanation for a similar scene in *I suppositi*
(the very scene, in fact, on which La Taille was to model
his own opening scene). There the Nurse, wishing to
discuss a delicate subject with the young Polinesta,
invites her to step outside where they cannot be over-
heard; for, she assures her, the beds, the cupboards and
even the doors in the house have ears. I suppose that a
modern reader of spy novels would readily accept the
argument that the safest place for airing one's secrets is
out of doors.

One other scene of *Les Corrivaus* may call for comment as far as its setting is concerned. It is not immediately clear why, in III.i, Jacqueline, after addressing a final remark to Restitue, should step outside the house. The Nurse follows her out into the street where they discuss Restitue's illness and her morals. Perhaps the explanation is that Jacqueline, having summoned the doctor, decides to wait for him outside the house. Such an interpretation could draw support from the fact that the doctor has not visited the house before, as his first remark in the next scene makes clear; he has, indeed, only recently arrived in the district (III.ii).

x   Characters

The motivation of characters is not explored in a very profound manner in Renaissance comedy, nor do they undergo a significant psychological development in the course of a play. Usually they possess some — but not necessarily all — of the salient features associated with certain types of persons (cf. the Section on 'Renaissance comedy' above). However, most authors avoid reproducing stereotypes and often try to create individuals by adding certain distinctive traits or by blending traditional ones in an original manner. Characters are also named, rather than being presented as mere types.

The *dramatis personae* of *Les Corrivaus* are briefly discussed below, under generic headings.

Young heroines

Although young girls, by the love they inspire, provide the central element for the plots of most Renaissance comedies, they make only rare and brief appearances on the stage. The reasons for this situation seem to be practical, ethical and social, rather than literary. In the first place, it has been suggested with some plausibility that the parts of the young heroines were generally kept small because they had to be performed by boys with only limited acting experience (until late in the sixteenth century, female characters used to be played by men or boys, who were often appropriately masked). A second, and doubtless even weightier, factor was once more the influence of the classical tradition, for female roles were rarely important in Roman comedies, the only girls portrayed there being young slaves who, though still virgins, were destined to become courtesans; no free-born girls were shown on the stage. And thirdly, the modest role played by girls in Renaissance comedy has been attributed at least in part to the relatively insignificant role which contemporary society assigned to women before marriage.[16]

Two young heroines figure in the plot of *Les Corri-vaus*. As has already been indicated (see Section vi), Restitue serves almost entirely the purposes of exposition and has no speaking part after the opening scene. As for Fleurdelys, who is the object of the young men's love and the cause of the rivalry from which the play takes its title, she is not seen at all by the audience. The latter must make do with the glowing description which Euvertre gives of her beauty (II.i) and with the warm if less poetically expressed praise of Fremin and Benard (IV.v, V.ii). The reason why Restitue appears on the stage and Fleurdelys does not should probably be sought in the convention which discouraged the portrayal of virgins in the learned comedy of the Renaissance.[17] This attitude was no doubt inspired by ethical (and religious) considerations not very dissimilar to those which had so severely limited female roles in Roman plays. Finally, it is typical of this type of comedy that neither Restitue nor Fleurdelys takes an active part in the development of the action.

Young men in love

Both Filadelfe and Euvertre have to overcome certain obstacles if they wish to win the girl they love. This is the situation in which the young man in love (the 'innamorato', to use the frequently employed Italian term) regularly finds himself. Euvertre's problem is a traditional one: opposition from an autocratic parent, in this case his own father who refuses his consent to the marriage, having set his miserly heart on a large dowry (II.i). The difficulties facing Filadelfe are more complex and in part less clearly defined. While La Taille's Prologue, echoing Boccaccio's text, indicates that both young men have been refused permission to marry Fleurdelys, there is no direct mention in the play itself of Filadelfe's father having objected to the match. There is, however, an implicit reference to his objection in Filadelfe's statement that his father's arrival in Paris will deprive him of any further opportunity to pursue his courtship (I.ii). Thus Benard's opposition, for which no reason is offered, supplies the motive for Filadelfe's decision to act as soon as possible. In addition, Filadelfe is confronted with the explicitly stated obstacle which is constituted by Fleurdelys's affectionate feelings towards Euvertre (I.i, II.i).

As is customary in Renaissance comedy, no physical descriptions are given of the young men. Indeed, all we know about Euvertre is that he is young and the son of Gerard Gontier. As far as his rival Filadelfe is concerned, we are merely told that he is a student — which is the status of many heroes of Renaissance comedy — and that he has been neglecting his academic subjects and physical training to devote himself to his amorous pursuits (I.i). Incidentally, the reference to the physical as well as the intellectual activities covered by Filadelfe's curriculum should remind us that humanistic education catered for the development of both the body and the mind, a fact of which any reader of Rabelais or Montaigne will already be well aware.

Parents

Much emphasis is placed in Renaissance comedies on the generation gap separating lovers from their parents. Benard and Gerard are labelled 'old men' in the list of *dramatis personae* and Jacqueline is described as an 'old lady' (of course, 'old' in sixteenth-century terminology need not mean more than what would to-day be regarded as average or advanced middle age). And although Fremin is simply identified at the outset by his place of origin, Picardy, any doubt that he belongs to the same age group is removed by his first conversation with Alizon (II.iii).

Except for Gerard's avarice — a vice frequently attributed to fathers in Renaissance comedy — the parents, compared to many portrayed in such plays, may well seem to us decidedly attractive characters, full of concern for their real or adoptive children (II.iii, III.i, IV.ii, etc.). Even Jacqueline's naïvety concerning her daughter's morals, which evokes ironic comment from the far more worldy-wise Nurse (III.i), has an endearing quality.

The ending shows the fathers at their most genial. Having arranged matters to their satisfaction, they decide to have some fun at the young men's expense; but Benard is soon carried away by his paternal love and tenderly embraces his son (V.vi). There are, moreover, none of those long censorious admonishments which one finds in similar circumstances in some contemporary plays, and the young men are not kept long in suspense regarding their 'punishment'.

Servants

The servants in *Les Corrivaus* conform fairly closely to the types commonly presented in Renaissance comedies. Gillet and Felippes, the menservants of Filadelfe and Euvertre, form a pair, fulfilling similar functions in the service of their young masters and possessing similar character traits. In particular, they miss no opportunity to stuff themselves with food and drink — Felix displays the same single-minded attention to his stomach — and they are ever ready to indulge in wenching (II.i, III.vi). Their bawdy approach to love and down-to-earth language serve as amusing contrasts to the romantic, idealizing attitude adopted by their masters. Starry-eyed petrarchism is thus balanced by licentious gauloiserie.

Gillet and Felippes also possess two other traits which are typical of many menservants in Renaissance comedy: they are given to bragging (I.iv, III.v); and they are cowards who put their own interests and safety above their duty towards their masters, whom they do not hesitate to abandon at the first sign of danger (see the same scenes).

Claude plays a somewhat different role in the play. He serves a man who is more advanced in years, and he may very well himself be older than Gillet and Felippes, since his principal function is to counterbalance the elderly Alizon — chiefly as a promoter of the young men's courtship. Like Alizon, he is quite prepared to betray his master and to expose the latter's daughter to an unpleasant experience. His and Alizon's motives are manifestly venal, notwithstanding their professions of altruism (I.iii, II.ii). Claude's help and complicity, like those of Alizon, are for sale.

As for Alizon, she is in the tradition of the bawds one so frequently encounters in humanist comedy. In addition to offering to admit Euvertre to the house, she tries to predispose Fleurdelys in his favour. There are also certain allusions to her being a procuress (see notes 12 and 13 to the play). Alizon's role in the play is altogether more important than Claude's, for she appears as well in two scenes with Fremin, which throw a revealing light on her relations with her employer. Being combative by nature — her pugnacity stands her in good stead in her quarrel with Claude — she is not afraid to argue with Fremin and to criticize his tardiness in finding a husband for Fleurdelys. She speaks her mind frankly and with a caustic wit which does not spare his declining faculties.

The role of the Nurse differs in certain essential respects from that of a chambermaid like Alizon. Attached to her young mistress since the latter's childhood, she enjoys an extremely close and warm relationship with her. It is significant that Restitue reveals her secret, not to her mother but to the Nurse; nor is Restitue's trust disappointed, for she promptly receives cheerful encouragement and useful advice. The Nurse is in no way distressed or outraged by the revelation of Restitue's conduct and of its result; indeed, she gives the impression of being morally unshockable. Her reaction is thus very different from the expressions of grief and the severe recriminations which the news will draw from Jacqueline (III.iv). The Nurse shrugs it all off with a saucy allusion to her own youth and quickly applies herself to finding a solution to the problem of how best to protect Restitue. For unlike Alizon, the Nurse is devoted to her young mistress — and, it may be noted, to her rather than to the mother by whom she is actually employed. Unlike Alizon, too, the Nurse is completely disinterested and unmercenary.

xi   Names

While most of the names do not appear to have any special significance, at least two have clearly been fashioned with special care. These are 'Filadelfe' and 'Fleurdelys'. The former is based on a compound Greek word meaning 'loving one's brother or sister. One might therefore observe facetiously that much confusion and misdirected love could have been avoided, if only some of the characters in the play had had some knowledge of the Greek language — which, after all, would not seem such an extraordinary accomplishment in a humanist comedy where even a servant like Felix knows all about Proserpina (IV.ii)! As for 'Fleurdelys', the choice of this poetic name accords well with Euvertre's lyrical comparison of the young girl's beauty to that of a flower blossoming in the warmth of the sun's rays (II.i). It is true that Euvertre likens her to a rose rather than to a lily (which 'lis' means), but then the rose has long been the flower symbolizing feminine beauty.

The choice of Fremin's name was not an arbitrary one either, for St. Firminus (or Firmin) was the first bishop of the diocese of Amiens, and Amiens is the capital city of Picardy, the province from which Fleurdelys's adoptive father is said to hail.[18]

A similar reason seems to underlie Boccacio's choice of 'Restituta' as the name for the heroine of *Decameron* V.vi. Boccaccio there tells the story of a beautiful girl who lived on the island of Ischia in the Bay of Naples. She is evidently named after St. Restituta, an African girl martyred at Carthage (in either 255 or 304 A.D.) and whose bones are said to be enshrined in the cathedral at Naples. St. Restituta was greatly venerated in Naples and also in Ischia. But if the name thus carries a local association in a tale partly set on the latter island, it does not produce a kindred effect in a play like *Les Corrivaus*, whose action takes place in Paris. Perhaps La Taille borrowed the name simply because he liked it. In any case, there can be little doubt that he took this unusual name from *Decameron* V.vi. He must have known the story well, since it follows the one which supplied him with the subject for his comedy.

Lastly, the name 'Euvertre' recalls that of St. Euvert (or Evortius) who was one of the saints specially venerated in Orléans. The fact that La Taille gave the name to one of his characters might indicate that he commenced work on the play while he was pursuing his legal studies in that city.

xii Conclusion

As mentioned earlier in this introduction, *Les Corrivaus* was written shortly before April 1562. It is thus one of the earliest French neo-classical comedies. Jodelle's *L'Eugène*, generally regarded as the first, preceded it by less than ten years.[19] Only three comedies are definitely known to have been written in the intervening period: *La Rencontre*, also by Jodelle, the text of which has not survived; and Grévin's *La Trésorière* and *Les Esbahis*, performed at the Collège de Beauvais in Paris in 1559 and 1561 respectively (Jodelle's plays had likewise been acted in university circles) and published in the latter year. To these may perhaps be added another comedy by Grévin, *La Maubertine*, since lost;[20] but little or nothing else.

The slow start made by French authors in creating a neo-classical comedy in the vernacular led Jacques Peletier du Mans, like Jodelle a member of the Pléiade, to express his disappointment at the unsatisfactory state of affairs in the *Art poëtique* he published in 1555. The Prologue to *Les Corrivaus* confirms that the situation had not greatly improved by 1562. La Taille's play was thus written in what might be termed the infancy of the French humanist comedy, which did not reach its most flourishing period until some fifteen years later. This especially applies to Italianate comedy, which was to receive a great boost from the establishment of Italian troupes in France in the early 1570's.

It is therefore not surprising that, despite the Pléiade's vociferous attacks on the literature of the preceding period, critics should have detected strong traces of mediaeval farce in a play such as *L'Eugène*. Revolutions seldom achieve immediately the complete break with the past which their rhetoric lays claim to. It has likewise been suggested[21] that the behaviour and the language of the servants in *Les Corrivaus* still reflect a considerable indebtedness to the same despised genre. However, while La Taille's play may well contain echoes of medi-aeval farce, it could be argued that his handling of the servants owes quite as much, if not more, to Latin and Italian models — thus, the idea for the ludicrous appear-ance of Gillet, equipped for fighting with kitchen utensils rather than in more traditional battle gear (III.iv) was almost certainly derived from a scene (V.i) in *Gl'ingannati*. In fact, one of the most striking aspects of *Les Corrivaus* is La Taille's great reliance on Italian sources. Not only did he take his subject from an Italian story, but he also drew extensively on at least two Italian plays (see Section iv above).

Les Corrivaus is the first (or, at any rate, the earliest surviving) French learned comedy to be written in prose, and the first to be based on Italian models. These facts will ensure that the play continues to receive close atten-tion from students of Renaissance drama; but they would hardly constitute sufficient reason for its being made available to a wider public in a translation like this one. Fortunately, the present publication can be justified on more appropriate grounds. *Les Corrivaus* is not one of those works which are likely to interest only the student of sources and influences or the scholar preoccupied with problems of literary history; it is a play of considerable intrinsic worth. *Les Corrivaus* is, indeed, a generally well-written and entertaining comedy which can still be read with pleasure to-day. It should appeal to all those interested in the theatre past and present.

Notes to the Introduction

It is assumed that many readers of this translation who have some difficulty in comprehending a play written in sixteenth-century French, may understand modern French or Italian.

Accordingly, reference will be made, in the notes and the bibliography, not only to critical studies in English, but also to certain particularly valuable publications in those other languages.

1   Details of the many editions and translations of Terence's comedies which were published in France during the Renaissance (and which were far more numerous than those of Plautus's plays) can be found in H.W. Lawton, *Contribution à l'histoire de l'humanisme . . . : Éditions et traductions.* (For the full titles of the works cited in abbreviated form in these notes, see the Bibliography, which also lists some easily accessible English translations of Plautus and Terence.)

2   One of the most brilliant Italian comedies, Giordano Bruno's *Il Candelaio* [*The Candle Bearer*] was actually first published in Paris (1582). Alamanni's *Flora*, though published in Italy, was written in France where the poet lived for many years.

3   The title is translated as *The Follies of Calandro* in Oliver Evans's English version (see Bibliography).

4   *Handbook of French Renaissance Dramatic Theory . . . ,.*

5   In his edition of *Les Corrivaus*, p.11.

6   For a modern English translation of this play, see *The Comedies of Ariosto . . .* , pp.99-158.

7   On La Taille's indebtedness to Le Maçon's translation, see especially L. Sozzi, 'Boccaccio in Francia . . . ', pp.338-43. D.L. Drysdall has reproduced Le Maçon's version of *Decameron* V.v in his edition of *Les Corrivaus*.

8   This is the English title given to the play in *The Comedies of Ariosto . . .*

9   For English translations of *Gl'ingannati*, which incidentally has long been considered a possible source of Shakespeare's *Twelfth Night*, see the Bibliography. Since it is not known which of the Intronati collaborated in the writing of the play, it is sometimes presented as being by an anonymous author (for instance, in *The Genius of the Italian Theater . . .*).

10   No copies appear to have survived of an earlier rendering or adaptation by Jacques Bourgeois (Paris, 1545), entitled *Comedie tres elegante en laquelle sont contenues les amours*

recreatives d'Erostrate . . . et de la belle Polymneste . . . (see R. Lebègue, 'Tableau . . . ', p.328; Alexandre Cioranesco, *Bibliographie de la littérature française du seizième siècle*, Paris: Klincksieck, 1959, p.150).

11 See R. Lebègue, 'Tableau. . .', pp.327-28. Lebègue does not explain that *Il sacrificio* was actually an allegorical playlet by the Intronati, which was first printed together with *Gl'ingannati* under the single title *Il sacrificio*. Since no copies of Estienne's 1543 edition have been found, it is not possible to say whether the volume contained a translation of both texts or simply of *Gl'ingannati*.

12 'Les Corrivaus' . . . , pp.15-21. See also L. Sozzi, 'Boccaccio in Francia . . . '.

13 *Contribution à l'histoire de l'humanisme . . . : Imitation et influence*, pp.108-17.

14 *Handbook of French Renaissance Dramatic Theory . . . *, pp.15-17.

15 P.205.

16 On the origin of the 'young girl in love' as a comedic type, see M. Lazard, *La Comédie humaniste . . . *, pp.66-70.

17 Fleurdelys is not the only heroine who never appears on the stage, even though the subject of her happiness constitutes an essential element of the plot. M. Lazard (*La Comédie humaniste . . . *, p.65) lists six other French Renaissance comedies where the same situation occurs.

18 Actually two saints of the same name are venerated at Amiens. Supposed by some writers to have been the first and third bishops of that city, they are considered by others to have been one and the same person.

19 *L'Eugène* has been dated at September 1552 by Jodelle's biographer Enea Balmas (*Un poeta del Rinascimento francese: Etienne Jodelle. La sua vita, il suo tempo*, Florence: Olschki, 1962, p.203).

20 See B. Jeffery, *French Renaissance Comedy . . . *, pp. 185-86.

21 Especially by L. Sozzi, 'Boccaccio in Francia . . .', pp. 345-46.

Select Bibliography

Translations of Latin and Italian Plays

Plautus: 'The Rope' and Other Plays, translated by E.F. Watling, Penguin Classics L136, 1964.
In addition to The Rope [Rudens], contains The Ghost [Mostellaria], A Three-Dollar Day [Trinummus], and Amphitryo.

Plautus: 'The Pot of Gold' and Other Plays, translated by E.F. Watling, Penguin Classics, 1965.
The 'other plays' are The Prisoners [Captivi], The Brothers Menaechmus [Menaechmi], The Swaggering Soldier [Miles gloriosus], and Pseudolus.

Three Plays by Plautus, translated and with an introduction by Paul Roche, Mentor Classic MY830, New American Library, 1968.
Contains Amphitryon [Amphitryo], Major Bullshot-Gorgeous [Miles gloriosus], and The Prisoners [Captivi].

Terence: 'The Brothers' and Other Plays, translated with an introduction by Betty Radice, Penguin Classics L156, 1965.
In addition to The Brothers [Adelphoe], contains The Eunuch [Eunuchus] and The Mother-in-Law [Hecyra].

Terence: 'Phormio' and Other Plays, translated with an introduction by Betty Radice, Penguin Classics L191, 1967.
Contains also The Girl from Andros [Andria] and The Self-Tormentor [Heauton timorumenos].

The Comedies of Ariosto, translated and edited by Edmond M. Beame and Leonard G. Sbrocchi, Chicago: University of Chicago Press, 1975.

Five Italian Renaissance Comedies, edited by Bruce Penman, Penguin Classics, 1978.
Contains Machiavelli, The Mandragola [La mandragola], tr. by Bruce Penman; Ariosto, Lena [La Lena],

tr. by Guy Williams; Aretino, *The Stablemaster* [*Il marescalco*], tr. by George Bull; *Gl'Intronati, The Deceived* [*Gl'ingannati*], tr. by Bruce Penman; Guarini, *The Faithful Shepherd* [Il pastor fido], tr. by Sir Richard Fanshawe.

The Genius of the Italian Theater, edited by Eric Bentley, Mentor Book MQ599, New American Library, 1964. Among the six plays are four from the Renaissance: Dovizi da Bibbiena, *The Follies of Calandro* [*Calandria*], tr. by Oliver Evans; Anonymous, *The Deceived* [*Gl'ingannati*] *Amyntas, tr. by Thomas Love Peacock; Tasso, [*Aminta*], tr. by Leigh Hunt; Bruno, *The Candle Bearer* [Il candelaio], tr. by J.R. Hale. *i.e. the play elsewhere attributed to the Accademici Intronati of Siena.

Studies

Chasles, Emile, 'Jean and Jacques de la Taille', in his *La Comédie en France au seizième siècle*, Paris: Didier, 1862, reprinted Geneva: Slatkine, 1969, pp.87-102.

Daley, Tatham Ambersley, *Jean de la Taille (1533-1608): Etude historique et littéraire*, Paris: Gamber, 1934.

Handbook of French Renaissance Dramatic Theory: A Selection of Texts, edited by H.W. Lawton, Manchester: Manchester University Press, 1949.

Herrick, Marvin T., *Comic Theory in the Sixteenth Century*, Urbana: University of Illinois Press, 1964.

Jeffery, Brian, *French Renaissance Comedy, 1552-1630*, Oxford: Clarendon Press, 1969.

Lawton, Harold Walter, *Contribution à l'histoire de l'humanisme en France: Térence en France au XVIe siècle. Éditions et traductions*, Paris: Jouve, 1926, reprinted Geneva: Slatkine, 1970.

Lawton, Harold Walter, 'Les Corrivaus de Jean de la Taille', in his *Contribution à l'histoire de l'humanisme en France: Térence en France au XVIe siècle*, Vol.II: *Imitation et influence*, Geneva: Slatkine, 1972, pp.108-17.

Lazard, Madeleine, *La Comédie humaniste au XVIe siècle et ses personnages*, Paris: Presses Universitaires de France, 1978.

Lebègue, Raymond, 'Tableau de la comédie française de la Renaissance', *Bibliothèque d'Humanisme et Renaissance*, VIII (1946), 278-344.

Lebègue, Raymond, *Le Théâtre comique en France de 'Pathelin' à 'Mélite'*, Paris: Hatier, 1972.

Sozzi, Lionello, 'Boccaccio in Francia nel cinquecento', in *Il Boccaccio nella cultura francese*, edited by Carlo Pellegrini, Florence: Olschki, 1971, pp.211-356 (see especially pp.334-46).

Toldo, Pierre, 'La Comédie française de la Renaissance', *Revue d'Histoire Littéraire de la France*, IV (1897), 366-92; V (1898), 220-64, 554-603; VI (1899), 571-608; VII (1900), 263-83. On *Les Corrivaus*, see V (1898), 559-63.

> For a detailed list of studies dealing with Jean de La Taille and his works, see D.L. Drysdall's edition of *Les Corrivaus*, pp.156-58.

The Rivals

(Les Corrivaus)

a comedy

Dramatis personae[1]

RESTITUE, a young girl

Her NURSE

FILADELFE
EUVERTRE } young men

CLAUDE
FELIPPES } servants

ALIZON, a chambermaid

BENARD,
GERARD } old men

FREMIN, a Picard

JACQUELINE, an old lady

The DOCTOR

FILANDRE, officer of the town watch

GILLET
FELIX } lackeys

Prologue

Seeing you all gathered here, gentlemen, one might suppose that you've all come to see a comedy. Well, I can assure you that you won't be disappointed. It's a true comedy that you'll be seeing, not a farce nor a morality. We don't waste our time on such low and foolish entertainments which merely show up the total ignorance of our French ancestors. The comedy which you are about to see is based and modeled on that favoured by the ancient Greeks and Romans and by some recent Italian authors; with this priceless jewel they enriched the already magnificent and splendid treasure of their tongues. If you appreciate beautiful things, I am certain that you will derive greater pleasure from a comedy of this kind than from any of the farces or moralities which you may have seen performed in our country until now. It is our earnest wish that such foolish trifles be banished from our kingdom, for they are like bitter spices which merely debase the fine flavour of our language. We propose to show you how much more agreeable and delightful is a comedy such as ours which has been composed with true art. It sounds no less graceful in our vernacular than Latin and Italian comedies do in theirs. In fact, I can justly claim that our language is to-day not at all inferior to theirs, when it comes to expressing ideas or to enriching and adorning a subject with eloquence. We are well aware that there are some persons who, with a frown and a shake of the

3

head, will dismiss comedy as being, in their opinion, a most vulgar type of work, even though it can be traced back to an author as illustrious as Terence. And they will furthermore declare that to write plays for the amusement of others is the mark of a man of low and base condition. To such persons we shall reply — assuming that they deserve any reply at all — that they know nothing about comedies composed with true art, for few of them are ever performed in France, mainly because we have hardly any authors like Plautus, Terence or Ariosto who, notwithstanding their eminence, did not disdain to write plays of this kind. If someone should remark that many of the plays being currently performed are described by their authors as 'comedies' or 'tragedies', I would retort that these designations are entirely inappropriate for such pitiful trifles which in no way preserve the character or style of the ancient drama. We therefore wish very much that our fellow-countrymen would stop watching and writing these wretched playlets and farces and moralities drawn from our native tradition, and that they would take the trouble to listen instead to well-constructed comedies composed, without affectation, in the manner of the ancients. I am certain that if we had properly understood this type of comedy and had realized what splendid entertainment it could provide, we would have adopted it long ago for our own use. Make an effort, therefore, from now on, to appreciate the excellence of such a comedy which has been misunderstood even by those who pass for scholars and has been attempted by only very few of the writers who are in some way acquainted with it. And then let us do what the Italians have done: let us imitate this comedy in our own language.

We have called our play *The Rivals*, because it is about two young men in love with the same girl. It will present to you, as if reflected in a mirror, the character and behaviour of the different types of persons in our society, such as old men, youths, servants, daughters of good families, and others. Listen carefully to what is being said, for if you don't, you'll lose the thread of the story and consequently derive only small pleasure and amusement from it. Still, so that you may follow the plot more easily, I will first provide you with a brief outline of it.

When the King, in preparation for his German campaign, sent his army into Lorraine and, in particular, to Toul, some of the inhabitants of the neighbouring city of Metz fled in fear and terror, since they could not tell what might be the intentions of our troops quartered so close-by.[2] Among them was a worthy widower by the name of Sieur Benard who escaped in great haste with his son, abandoning all his possessions and even leaving his small daughter behind in his house, either because the child was sick or because he had forgotten all about her in his panic, or through some other unfortunate circumstance. He had, in any case, only these two children: the son, who was called Filadelfe, and the daughter, whose name was Fleurdelys. The girl was soon afterwards carried off by a soldier named Fremin who had entered Metz with the Constable's army. He felt such compassion for her that he took her back with him to his home in Picardy, where he brought her up as his own daughter. Some time later he left Picardy because of the wars which were so constantly raging there, and settled with his adopted daughter here in Paris, so that he might spend his remaining days in peace and tranquillity. In the meantime, Benard de Metz, as he was called, had returned home after his flight. And when he discovered that he had lost not only his possessions but also his daughter, he was seized by fear that the wars, which were continuing all the time, might cost him still further suffering in future, including the loss of his only remaining child. He therefore sent his son to Paris to stay with a wealthy widow by the name of Dame

Jacqueline whom he had known for a long time; and he planned to settle here himself, once he had put his affairs in order. His son Filadelfe had no sooner set foot in his hostess's house than he fell head over heels in love with her daughter Restitue. To cut a long story short, he played his cards so well from the outset that he obtained from her what he most desired, whereupon his great passion began to cool. And gradually he abandoned his mistress in favour of a new love, for he had now set all his affection on a young girl who lived next door and whom everyone took to be the daughter of a Picard. I won't tell you who she really was; you'll find that out at the end of the play. Anyway, she was loved not only by Filadelfe but also by another handsome and charming young man called Euvertre. Both were refused permission to marry her for various apparently good reasons, and so they both resolved to possess her by whatever means were most expedient. The Picard had in his household an elderly chambermaid called Alizon and a servant by the name of Claude. Filadelfe became very friendly with Claude who promised to admit him into the house on the first occasion when Restitue's father went out for a longer period; Filadelfe would then be free to deal as he wished with the girl he loved. Euvertre, for his part, ingratiated himself by means of presents and entreaties so successfully with the chambermaid that she promised him the same thing as had been promised to Filadelfe, and in addition she predisposed her mistress in his favour. You must understand that neither young man knew of the other's plans; each held unsuspectingly to his arrangements and waited for the father to leave the house on some business. And this, the devil take it, is as much as I can tell you, for here comes Restitue who gave herself so generously to Filadelfe. She has just revealed a secret to her nurse. Listen, and you'll hear all about it. Fare well, all of you.

ACT I

SCENE I   RESTITUE (a young girl), NURSE

RESTITUE: Dear Nurse, now you know the whole secret of my heart and the full cause for my grief. I finally had to reveal them to you; even if I tried, I could not hide anything from you. As you can see, the matter is of great importance to me, for it affects my honour and perhaps even my life. Don't be surprised therefore that I've waited so long before telling you and have kept you in suspense until this moment; indeed, I'll ask you to keep it a strict secret even now, so that nobody can possibly suspect that you know about it. You can then help me in my need.

NURSE: Why, there's no one with whom your secret will be safer than with your nurse. But I'm not surprised any more that you should have been so reluctant to tell me about it. Really, Restitue, I couldn't understand why all you did this past month was to lament and grieve, and to weep so loudly that your sobs must surely have been heard from one end of the city to the other. One minute you appeared to be on the point of telling me something, the next you'd thought better of it, and you went on changing your mind and changing it back again a hundred times a day. When I remembered the merry life we had led in days gone by, I thought that you had decided to turn yourself into a nun or a saint, or into a true Mary

7

Magdalene. To be sure, the world has always held
you in high esteem. 'She's the most virtuous of girls,'
they all say, 'the most chaste, the most this and the
most that. She never laughs, she never leaves her
house, she never falls in love.' But I can see now that
the truth is quite different. No wonder you didn't
dare tell me straightaway about your nine-months'
illness! But come now, Restitue, that's no reason for
tears and sadness. All right, so you're going to have a
child! Good Lord, your world will surely not come to
an end because of it. Holy Mary, we were all young
once and fell in love like everyone else. When I was
sixteen, I had my frilly frocks just like you and
probably had them just as stuffed as yours is,[3] but
that never caused me such frenzies of despair as
you've fallen into.

RESTITUE: Ah, cursed be the day . . .

NURSE: What's the good of all this weeping and wailing?
You'd do much better, my fine lady, to explain to me
fully through whom, when and how you let the cat
get at the cheese.[4]

RESTITUE: In the first place, you ought to know that this is
Filadelfe's doing.

NURSE: The young man who is staying in our house?

RESTITUE: The same.

NURSE: But how did it happen? Tell me, do.

RESTITUE: He had no sooner come to live with us, as he
had been instructed to do by his father Benard on
leaving Metz, than he fell in love with me.

NURSE: Fancy my not noticing anything!

RESTITUE: Such was his love that in no time at all he'd
lost interest in his studies and in the practice of
arms and the other pursuits gentlemen engage in,
and instead he made me his sole concern and centre
of attention. As a result, he spent most of his time in

conversation alone with me . . . But why do you want me to tell you all this? Why should I describe all my troubles to you, since it's too late for remedies?

NURSE: Well now, if he came alone to your room and even right into your bed, as seems to have been the case, is that any reason for despair? These are nothing but the little follies of love which you probably committed without giving them a second thought. Only you must make sure that your mother doesn't find out about them, or anybody else, for that matter.

RESTITUE: That's just why I wanted to ask you to help me and also arrange for me to be soon rid of this child.[5]

NURSE: I'll do what I can. But tell me, didn't you agree to get married, the two of you?

RESTITUE: What?

NURSE: I ask because it mightn't be such a bad arrangement, if matters come to a head, for you to be married to this Filadelfe. Your honour would then be protected from any stains by the cloak of matrimony. Now why are you shaking your head? Don't tell me you never thought of getting his promise!

RESTITUE: No, I didn't. It never occurred to me to speak to him about it. But even if he had promised me, what good would that do me now?

NURSE: You mean he could just deny everything, because there weren't any witnesses? or that since he isn't a Parisian, he could take himself off whenever he liked?

RESTITUE: No, I wouldn't be afraid of that happening. My dear Nurse, leave Paris is the last thing he's likely to do, and I've good reason to be sure of that. He won't stir from this city for the rest of his life, and yet there isn't a chance that he'll marry me. So you can see how far off the mark you are.

NURSE: But how can you be so certain? After all, he's only staying in Paris for a while. His home is in Metz in Lorraine, where his father is still living.

RESTITUE: Then you haven't heard? When Filadelfe arrived he brought my mother a letter from his father, in which Benard announced that he planned to settle here for good with his son, as soon as he had sold his property and completed certain lawsuits he was engaged in.

NURSE: Really? But why should Benard wish to leave his home town?

RESTITUE: Is that really so surprising? He's getting on in years, he's a widower, and for many years now he's been living under war conditions. Surely it's only natural that he should want to move to a peaceful, pleasant and safe city, rather than remain in Metz where the wars have been causing him such hardship. According to Filadelfe, he even lost his daughter through them, when our troops entered the town.

NURSE: I can understand how he must feel, then. But, in that case, what should prevent you from marrying your Filadelfe?

RESTITUE: Don't you know how falsely he's acted towards me? and that he's abandoned me and given all his love to the daughter of the Picard who lives next door to us?

NURSE: You mean to Fleurdelys, the daughter of Sieur Fremin — that man who left his province because of the wars, to come and live here in Paris?

RESTITUE: That's the one. Filadelfe is in love with his daughter, and that makes me really furious. If at least he were her only suitor! But from what I've heard, there are others, among them a young man from our own city called Euvertre, who is the son

of Sieur Gerard. They say that he loves her quite as much as Filadelfe does and is better loved by her in return. Just think, Nurse, what great wrong he's doing me!

NURSE: So that's what Gillet, that good-for-nothing servant of his, was babbling about when he'd had a good deal to drink and after we'd made up our usual quarrel. He was complaining about always having to be on the run, trotting here and there, and more often than not being sent with messages to Claude, the servant of Fleurdelys's father. Filadelfe has obviously made a contact there to help him in his affair. I'd quite forgotten about it until your remark reminded me of it.

RESTITUE: Tell me frankly, then: have I any reason to want to be married to Filadelfe?

NURSE: No, you haven't. All the same, there's no point in your fretting when nothing is lost yet. I'm sure I can find a way to save both your honour and your child.

RESTITUE: But how?

NURSE: Tell your mother, Dame Jacqueline, that you're not feeling very well.

RESTITUE: That's true enough.

NURSE: And that you would like to enjoy the country air for a while. I'm sure that she will, as usual, send you, with me to look after you, to your farm 'Bellair', not four miles from here.

RESTITUE: And what shall we do there?

NURSE: We'll find a thousand ways for you to be rid of your child. I'll show you a marvellous solution I know.

RESTITUE: I'll do as you suggest. Now we must choose the right moment to speak to my mother.

NURSE: Look, isn't that the young man we've just been talking about? I'm certain he's up to something, for he hasn't been in the house all day.

RESTITUE: Please don't take any notice of him!

SCENE II   FILADELFE (alone)

FILADELFE: Alas, I realize very well, Restitue, even without your emphasizing the point by avoiding me, that I am doing you wrong in paying court to another girl. But truly, is there anyone who is not aware of Cupid's power? and who doesn't know that Cupid is blind, young and fickle, uncontrollable and deaf to reason? Because of him, I'm as restless as if I were walking on quicksilver, and as a result I've been running all over Paris looking for Claude, my cruel mistress's servant, in the hope of having some news of her. I must keep on good terms with this lackey, for he could be of great help to me in my courtship and serve as a trustworthy messenger. But I must make my move soon, as my father will be arriving shortly. His presence here will put an end to all my chances of pursuing my courtship. But there's an even stronger reason why I should lose no more time: I have a rival whom I must keep ahead of at all costs, or else he'll possess my darling Fleurdelys before I ever can. Good, here comes the fellow I've been looking for.

SCENE III   CLAUDE, FILADELFE

CLAUDE: There he is at last, thank God!

FILADELFE: Well, Claude, what news do you bring me?

CLAUDE: The best possible. This is the day you've been longing for.

FILADELFE: How so?

CLAUDE: I've persuaded my master to go out to-day. Before another hour is up, I shall admit you to where you'll find your beloved Fleurdelys.

FILADELFE: How happy that makes me!

CLAUDE: The rest of the arrangements are up to you.

FILADELFE: They're already made. Two friends have promised to help me; as for me, I'm going over there straightaway and shall be waiting in the alley, ready to go inside as soon as you open the door. But how will you let me know when your master has gone out?

CLAUDE: I'll signal to you from the back door which I'll leave unbolted for you.

FILADELFE: What signal will you use?

CLAUDE: I'll make three circles in the air with a torch I'll be holding. That will be the signal for you to enter.

FILADELFE: Will there be anyone in the house who could disturb me?

CLAUDE: You needn't worry, there's only Alizon, the old chambermaid. I'll easily find a way to get rid of her.

FILADELFE: That's all right then. In the meantime, I'll take up my position in the lane, where my friends will join me. Don't forget those presents I promised you, Claude, though I could never repay you as you deserve for all the help you've given me.

CLAUDE: Please say no more about it. The only favour I ask in return is that you act discreetly and do everything possible so that no-one will ever suspect that I played any part in the affair, either through consenting or helping. I'll be playing the innocent for all I'm worth, full of amazement and surprise, when you enter the room where Fleurdelys will be.

FILADELFE: I've already told you that I shall keep it all a secret.

CLAUDE: Otherwise I shall be ruined and done for, I swear it. Every time my master leaves just to go into town for a short while, he reminds us a thousand times to take good care of his daughter.

FILADELFE: Have you spoken to Fleurdelys about me?

CLAUDE: Certainly not. It would be a mistake, I'm sure, if I were to mention your love to her, for she wouldn't take the matter seriously.

FILADELFE: But whyever not? Am I so unattractive or lacking in grace that she couldn't love me? Or am I so different in character and temperament from her that we couldn't live in harmony together?

CLAUDE: I certainly can't see any difference. In fact, if I hadn't heard you say that you were an only child, I'd have taken her for your sister, for she resembles you remarkably.[6] Anyway, do you have anything else for me to do?

FILADELFE: No. But have you seen my servant? I sent him to look for you three hours ago.

CLAUDE: No, I haven't seen him.

FILADELFE: I expect he's busy swilling wine somewhere.

SCENE IV   GILLET (lackey to Filadelfe), FILADELFE

GILLET: Really, I'd be an utter fool, with my master leading such an amorous life, if I didn't get in on the action myself. But I'd never do it his way, for he's one of those moonstruck lovers who stick to one mistress and dilly-dally for two or three years and in the end never get anywhere with her. When he sent me to look for Claude to-day, I did a fine bit of love-making.[7]

FILADELFE (aside): There's my lackey. I'll stay back here for a minute, so that I can overhear what he says.

GILLET: When I didn't meet my man straightaway, I made post-haste for that tavern near-by.

FILADELFE (*aside*): Just as I thought. My God, I'll punish you soundly for that.

GILLET: When I got there, I first of all downed some six or seven pints, and after that I made my way to the kitchen, where I feel even more in my element than a salamander in fire.[8] And in the kitchen I found the landlord's chambermaid who's a real beauty.

FILADELFE (*aside*): An admirable girl, for sure!

GILLET: She really caught my fancy. And, to make a long story short, we put our equipment together. I can't imagine a chambermaid so haughty and stuck-up that she'd dare turn down a man like me, even if I say so myself.

FILADELFE (*aside*): What a coxcomb he is!

GILLET: It's just not in my nature to devote myself to one saint at a time. When I see breeches that match my doublet, I make a grab at them. After all, hasn't a mouse more than one hole to run into? By God, that's the proper way to act! I'm not one for wasting my time like some lovers in Lent who alchemize love and extract its quintessence. They only feed on idle fancies and always finish up clutching a handful of wind.[9]

FILADELFE (*aside*): A worthy thought, well suited to a ruffian like you.

GILLET: There's my master! I'll change my tune without letting on that I've seen him.

FILADELFE: Come here, you rascal! Where have you been?

GILLET: Where you sent me, sir.

FILADELFE: Did you meet Claude?

GILLET: Yes.

15

FILADELFE: You're a lying rogue! He told me just now that he hadn't seen you. (*Aside*) This gallant fellow never stirs from the tavern. By God, I'm going to give him such . . . But there's another matter I must see to first. Now he's made me forget what I wanted to say to him. I've so many things on my mind, I don't know where to begin. Ah yes, I remember.—Go and find Camille and François, and tell them that the day and hour have come for the business we discussed the other day. They should meet me in the lane by Fremin's house and bring all the necessary implements with them. Run along! What are you waiting for? What are you muttering about, you scoundrel? Wait! (*Aside*) I'd be a great fool to entrust a message to this drunkard. —I'd better go myself. But mind you join me in the lane in a short while. Only first find yourself some weapons, so that you won't be completely useless to me if there should be a fight.[10]

GILLET: Don't worry, sir, you can rely on me. God knows, there's no braver man than me. Believe me, I'll never be the last in the fray, for I'll be the first to run if the fight goes against us.[11]

ACT II

SCENE I EUVERTRE (a young man), FELIPPES (his servant)

EUVERTRE: Alas, why must men be so obsessed with material things? Why are virtue, great beauty, and nobility of character so little esteemed unless they are accompanied by riches? Why are precious stones, diamonds, rubies and emeralds — to which I would compare my Fleurdelys's marvellous qualities — so little prized unless they are mounted in gold? Is a woman without wealth not preferable to wealth without a woman?

FELIPPES: Well, Euvertre, what did you want me for?

EUVERTRE: You've come at the right moment. I've sent someone to look for you.

FELIPPES: What were you lamenting about just now?

EUVERTRE: My father's miserliness.

FELIPPES: Why, what's he done?

EUVERTRE: I'll tell you, and then you'll also understand what I need you for.

FELIPPES: Go on.

EUVERTRE: You should know, in the first place, that I'm in love with a fifteen-year old girl who is virtuous and a marvel of grace and physical perfection.

With every passing day, she grows still more beautiful and delightful, like a rose blossoming and
unfolding its leaves under the warmth of the sun's
rays. Her name is Fleurdelys and she is the daughter
of Sieur Fremin, a Picard who has recently settled in
this city? Perhaps you know her?

FELIPPES: Of course I do! She's also being ardently courted
by Filadelfe, a neighbour of this Picard.

EUVERTRE: I'm well aware of that.

FELIPPES: So what's to be done? Shall we break his neck?

EUVERTRE: Wait till you hear the rest. Ever since the day,
some two months ago, when I fell in love with this
girl, I've tried by all possible means to possess her. I
was even ready to marry her. But you know what a
miserly and stingy man my father is! When he found
out that Fleurdelys's father was not very well off,
having spent much of his wealth in the wars, he
absolutely refused his consent and was very angry
with me. He insisted that I was still too young and
that it was too early for me to be thinking of
marriage. That's what I was lamenting over just
now. However, since my father won't budge from
his position, I'm determined now to possess the girl
in any way I can.

FELIPPES: What do you mean?

EUVERTRE: Well, Fremin, the girl's father, has an old
chambermaid in his household.

FELIPPES: You mean Alizon?

EUVERTRE: Yes.

FELIPPES: She's a rare old crone, that one! But go on, go
on.

EUVERTRE: I've so ingratiated myself with her through
presents, entreaties and various kindnesses, that
she's passed on some messages from me to my

darling Fleurdelys and has made her feel well-disposed and friendly towards me. And just a week ago she told me that, in order to bring matters to a head, she would admit me to the house during one of Fremin's absences and that once I was inside and had found Fleurdelys, I would be free to do as I wished. My mind's therefore made up: if Fleurdelys doesn't accede to my wishes, I shall carry her off by force.

FELIPPES: Listen, Euvertre . . .

EUVERTRE: What is it now? Don't try to dissuade me, for I won't change my mind.

FELIPPES: All right, then, do as you please. But what do you need me for?

EUVERTRE: This morning Alizon sent me word through my lackey that she wished to speak to me. No doubt she wants to let me know that her master is going out. To-day would be ideal, since my father is out of town. That's why I sent for you to meet me here near Fremin's house. Will you help me abduct the girl, if that should be necessary?

FELIPPES: Yes, all right. But can we manage by ourselves?

EUVERTRE: My friend Calixte has promised to help me. We must go to his house which is close to Fremin's, and then we'll be ready whenever Alizon opens the door for us. He's also undertaken to find weapons for the three of us.

FELIPPES: I won't let you down if I can help it, since that's the situation. But can we be sure of success? Is there no-one who could spoil our plan?

EUVERTRE: Who the devil should there be? It's true that I have a rival in the gallant Filadelfe. But how can he interfere when he's not even aware of our little plot?

FELIPPES: In any case, I swear he'd be no match for us, if we should ever come up against him. Believe me, he has no more chance of marrying Fleurdelys than if he were her brother.

EUVERTRE: I can see Alizon coming out of her house. Go and wait for me at Calixte's. I think I know what she wants to tell me.

FELIPPES: I intend to enjoy myself to-day while that feeble-minded old master of mine has gone for a stroll in the country. We'll spend more money in a single hour than he earns in a whole month.

SCENE II   ALIZON (a chambermaid), EUVERTRE

ALIZON: Heaven knows what misfortunes I'm likely to suffer to-day, after that frightful dream I had last night! Every time I have such a nightmare, I meet with some fresh calamity or vexation. And yet I've heard people say that it's foolish to believe in such things.

EUVERTRE: What are you muttering about, Alizon? Are you calculating how long it still is to Low Sunday? Or are you meditating on the lives of the saints or on the wounds of St. Francis?[12]

ALIZON: Not at all; I came out to look for you, Euvertre, since I'd sent you word this morning to meet me.

EUVERTRE: Well, what do you have to tell me?

ALIZON: My master will shortly be going into town.

EUVERTRE: That's wonderful news? But how will you admit me to where I can find my dear Fleurdelys?

ALIZON: I'll open the back door to signal to you by waving my spindle three times in a circle. You'll know then that it's time for you to go in through that door.

EUVERTRE: Splendid! I'll be waiting in a friend's house near-by. But I'm afraid that someone in the house might spoil my plan. Isn't there a servant called Claude in your household? I'd be mighty glad not to see him around.

ALIZON: Don't worry about him, I'll get rid of him easily enough. In any case, he'll have to go out to fetch our master.

EUVERTRE: If you help me in this affair, Alizon, I know where I can lay my hands on the most richly decorated belt and the most beautiful pair of rosaries you ever saw in your life. I'll give them to you, and many other presents too.

ALIZON: Oh, that's really not necessary. I'll only ask you once again to keep the whole thing secret, so that Fremin doesn't suspect me of having had a hand in it.

EUVERTRE: Come now, I've already sworn it many times. But after what you've just told me, I must quickly set about making my arrangements. There's no time to waste!

ALIZON: Hurry up then! Look, Fremin's already leaving.

SCENE III   FREMIN (a Picard), ALIZON

FREMIN: Alizon, while I'm in town, you take good care of Fleurdelys, do you hear? And don't budge from the house! All things considered, I'd rather stay at home, if only this business weren't so urgent. I have a premonition that something unpleasant is going to happen. But no matter what occurs, don't let her leave the house.

ALIZON: Really, Sieur Fremin, if you had listened to me you'd have been free of all fear and concern for your daughter long ago, for you could easily have arranged a very good match for her, as I suggested. Well, you had your own way in the matter, and that's fine. But who do you think you're going to marry her to, anyway — a prince, perhaps?

FREMIN: Do you imagine I would have waited so long if I could have arranged a suitable marriage for her? Still, as you know, I'm constantly receiving proposals, including one from Euvertre, the son of that wealthy merchant Gerard Gontier. But his father has roundly refused his consent.

ALIZON: You must do as you think best. Frankly, though, I think you've been starving her of love for too long.

FREMIN: You fancy that all women are like you — you know what I mean.

ALIZON: And you, on the other hand, imagine that everybody is as cold as you are.

FREMIN: It's true that I don't get as worked up about love as you'd like me to.

ALIZON: My poor man, you're hardly up to it any more. And if you do still indulge yourself, it's so rare that it barely counts.

FREMIN: Enough of that! If anyone should ask for me, tell him that I've gone to call on Captain Chandiou and that I shall be back soon.

ACT III

SCENE I   JACQUELINE (an old lady), NURSE

JACQUELINE: Cheer up, Restitue, I want you to get better just as much as you do, so mind you wrap up warmly in bed.

NURSE: I think you're very wise, Dame Jacqueline, to allow her to enjoy the country air with me for a while. She really is feeling quite ill.

JACQUELINE: I have no objection at all to her going. In fact, if I weren't expecting Filadelfe's father to arrive any day now, I would have gone with her myself. But it worries me that I don't know exactly why she is so poorly.

NURSE: Isn't it obvious, though? To live all the time in a city, with no opportunity for amusement but being forever shut up in a room or else in church praying to God - surely that's enough to make anybody ill.

JACQUELINE: May God keep her safe! I should be very sad if the poor girl were to be seriously ill; for quite apart from her being my only child, I don't mind telling you, since she can't hear us at present, that she's the most virtuous girl in the whole world: she's not dissolute, and her conduct doesn't give rise to scandal, like that of so many other girls; and she doesn't spend her time with young men, as our neighbours' daughters apparently do — instead, she is always praying or at her devotions. Truly, she leads the life of a saint.

NURSE: How right you are! And she's enjoying the fruits of virtue. Those who know her intimately can testify to that.

JACQUELINE: Here's the doctor I've sent for to examine her before she leaves for the country, since it isn't easy to find a doctor there.

NURSE (*aside*): The devil take him! I'm afraid things are going to turn out badly for me.

SCENE II DOCTOR, JACQUELINE, NURSE

DOCTOR: From the directions that boy gave me, the house should be in this neighbourhood. Perhaps this is the lady I'm to call on.

JACQUELINE: Yes, indeed, doctor.

DOCTOR: You sent for me. Tell me, what can I do for you?

JACQUELINE: I'd like you to examine my daughter who is unwell. I'm thinking of sending her to the country, and I want you therefore to tell me exactly what is wrong with her, so that she can benefit fully from the treatment you prescribe for her.

NURSE (*aside*): May God strike the doctor blind or my mistress deaf!

DOCTOR: What does she complain of?

JACQUELINE: Just loss of appetite, and she also suffers occasionally from stomach pains, fainting fits, and colic.

DOCTOR: That doesn't sound too serious. But I can't give you a definite diagnosis until I've examined her, and also her urine, if necessary.

JACQUELINE: I quite understand. Do come in.

DOCTOR: Let's go in, then. Confound it, I've forgotten my spectacles.

NURSE (*alone*): Don't let that stop you from going in. She's big enough for you to see her without them — much too big, in fact. But here I'm joking, and I don't really feel in the least like it. The good doctor is bound to declare her pregnant the minute he sees her. He was summoned so suddenly and unexpectedly, I haven't had a chance to put him in the picture. And then he's only recently arrived in this district and doesn't know the girl. He'll assume that she's married and that he ought to tell the truth. Still, whatever may happen, I'm going in anyway to see what he'll do.

SCENE III   CLAUDE, ALIZON

CLAUDE: I can't see a soul in the street, so I'm going to give Filadelfe the signal we've arranged.

ALIZON: I must let Euvertre know that Claude and Fremin have gone out.

CLAUDE: I've already opened the back door for them.

ALIZON: I've just noticed that our back door has very conveniently been left unbolted.

CLAUDE: Who's that talking back there? Damn, it's that old witch Alizon! May the devil dash her brains out! She'll spoil everything.

ALIZON: Isn't that Claude over there? Heaven help me, he'll upset all my arrangements.

CLAUDE: I must find a way to get rid of her quickly. — What on earth are you doing here?

ALIZON: What are you doing here yourself?

CLAUDE: What are you going to do with that spindle?

ALIZON: And you, what are you going to do with that torch?

CLAUDE: I need it to fetch my master.

ALIZON: Why don't you go and fetch him then, instead of wandering about here?

CLAUDE: And you — why aren't you weaving with your spindle at our neighbour's house as usual?

ALIZON: I don't feel like it.

CLAUDE (*aside*): My God, I'm sure this woman will make me . . . —Come, Alizon, I really don't want to get angry with you. Do as I say and just go away.

ALIZON: And I'm telling you, Claude, that I'll do nothing of the sort.

CLAUDE: So you won't leave, you old witch?

ALIZON: No, I won't, you miserable scoundrel!

CLAUDE: Easy now! Didn't you use to be a maid of all trades — you get my meaning?[13]

ALIZON: How dare you? You're a foul liar, I was nothing of the kind. By God, I'll make you take back those words!

CLAUDE: All right, we'll say no more about it. It's below my dignity to swap insults with you, anyway. I'm asking you again, Alizon, go away and leave me alone here.

ALIZON: Go away yourself!

CLAUDE: If you ever make me let go of the handle of this torch . . .

ALIZON: As God is my witness, if you come any closer, I'll give you such a clout with my spindle . . .

CLAUDE: Damnation! If you put me in a rage, I'll break that thick stupid head of yours! (*Aside*) But I'm even more stupid myself to be wasting my time with her. Why the devil should I worry about her? Why should I put off what I've arranged to do, just because of her?

ALIZON: He's off at last. May he be hung by his neck! He
    must be up to some devilry, he was so anxious to get
    rid of me. Still, I must let him get a little further away
    before I give my signal.

SCENE IV   NURSE, ALIZON

NURSE: Confound this worthy doctor and all the other
    doctors in the world! A curse on their tribe! Didn't I
    say he'd be sure to tell the mother that her daughter
    was pregnant? I winked at him, I made signs at him
    with my fingers, I stepped on his foot — all in vain.
    That's no doubt put an end to our little scheme to get
    away to the country.

ALIZON: I wonder what that woman is wailing about.
    Good God alive, what's all that noise in our house?
    It sounds as if a whole crowd is coming in through
    the back door. Can that be Euvertre? But I haven't
    given him the signal yet. I'd better go and see what
    all the racket is about. Heavens, I can hear Fleurdelys
    shouting for help.

NURSE: How I wish I could lay my hands on Filadelfe! I'd
    love to give him a piece of my mind and tell him
    about the fine scandal he's caused in our house.
    What a pitiful spectacle they make: that poor girl,
    moaning and tearing her hair; and her mother,
    weeping, shouting, raging, heaping reproaches on
    her daughter and demanding to know who's brought
    this dishonour on her. If her lover at least hadn't
    abandoned her! Ah, Restitue, Restitue, your fate is a
    sound warning to all the other young ladies to
    beware of those dainty-faced and smooth-complex-
    ioned young men in the flower of their youth, for
    their passions quicken and die as a straw fire.
    They're like those huntsmen who furiously pursue
    their prey over mountains, through forests and

across valleys, and once they've captured it, lose all interest in it. These young men act just like them: when they have conquered you, ladies, and have obtained from you what they desired most, they forsake you; and then you're left lamenting that you've been reduced from mistresses to slaves. I'm not suggesting that you should renounce love; I'm only warning you to beware of those beardless youths who are so fickle and inconstant, and am advising you to pick fruit that is neither green and sour, nor already overripe . . . Good heavens, where's this fellow running in such a panic, with a spit in his hand and a tin-pot helmet on his head?

SCENE V   GILLET, NURSE

GILLET: Who would want to stay there, in God's name, among all those naked swords?

NURSE: Why, it's Gillet! So much the better; now I'll know what's happened to his master.

GILLET: Anyone who wants to join in is welcome to! As for me, I'm clearing out and will go back later. Damn it all, a fellow must look after his own skin. Why should I let myself be beaten black and blue, for God's sake? And then, these crazy young lovers lash out at you without so much as an 'On your guard', confound them!

NURSE: I wonder if he's still angry with me because of those insults we exchanged in the kitchen after supper last night and which got us so mad at each other. — Hey Gillet, where've you been with that spit?

GILLET: Where've I been? You may well ask! I've been in the devil of a fight. You should have seen how I hit them and struck them and beat them and knocked them to the ground! I'd have impaled one of them alive if he hadn't run away.

NURSE: But tell me what this is all about and why you're armed like this.

GILLET: No, you can't keep a secret.

NURSE: Yes, I can, believe me.

GILLET: All right then. My master Filadelfe . . .

NURSE: Where is your master? A curse on him! I wish he'd broken his neck and legs the first time he set foot in our house, seeing what a great scandal he's created here.

GILLET: Why? What's he done? What is it? What's going on?

NURSE: I'll tell you later. Just finish what you were saying, so I know where he is.

GILLET: There's not much to tell. He got the signal, we rushed into the house, he seized the girl around the waist, she cried out, some old woman appeared from God knows where and yelled even louder. At their screams another young man came charging along and tried to stop us, there was a fight and I made off.

NURSE: I don't understand a word of what you're saying. But one thing is clear: you ran away like a coward and probably left your master in the lurch.

GILLET: My good woman, you don't understand military tactics. Don't you know that a quick and successful retreat is better than a bungled delaying action?

NURSE: Is that so? Just now you were setting yourself up as Captain Courageous.

GILLET: It's a waste of time talking to you, for you've no idea how wars are conducted.

NURSE: Hey, you're a real whippersnapper!

GILLET: Whippersnapper! By God, I've a good mind to stick this spit right though you. But, come to think of it, the flesh isn't worth roasting. Now just where are those cowards who attacked my master? What wouldn't I do to them if they were here! By heaven, I'd ... Dear God, isn't that one of them coming this way now? I'm lost. He's looking for me. Where can I hide? Saint Thomas, I beseech you, save me.

NURSE: What's got into you? Only a moment ago you were so full of courage!

SCENE VI   FELIPPES, GILLET, NURSE

FELIPPES: Thank God, I've given those odious constables the slip! (*To the other prisoners*) That's right, you stay put, don't run away! You see if they don't march you smartly off to prison.

GILLET:Why, if it isn't my friend Felippes, Gerard's servant! I won't rest until I've made things up with him.

FELIPPES: Oh, it's you Gillet. Tell me, fine sir, didn't I see you fighting against my young master Euvertre just now? I've a good mind to . . .

NURSE: Come, don't hold it against him. After all, he was one of the first to run away.

GILLET: I didn't run away, I tell you — I simply retreated. Am I wrong, Felippot,[14] or did you do the same?

FELIPPES: Come, give me your hand! You're a good friend.

GILLET: But what has happened to our masters? What was the result of their quarrel and their fight?

FELIPPES: They're both being marched off to prison and Claude, Fremin's servant, too, so help me God.

NURSE: Filadelfe's in prison? But why?

GILLET: Yes, tell us how it happened.

FELIPPES: Well, when my master and I got the sign from Alizon, the chambermaid,[15] we rushed into Fremin's house and tried to get Fleurdelys away from your master who had seized hold of her. He and Euvertre fought furiously and they made such a fearful din with their swords that the neighbours became very angry, thinking we were trying to rape the girl in public, and started to throw stones and torches. All this noise somehow brought out Filandre, the officer of the watch, and his constables, and he arrested all three of them and marched them off to jail or to his house, I'm not sure which. The others who had been helping Euvertre or your master scattered in all directions.

NURSE: So at least no one was hurt?

FELIPPES: No, thank God.

GILLET: In that case I'm not going to worry my head about it any more. Really, I believe one shouldn't take these matters too much to heart. There's nothing more harmful, says Nostradamus, for people who want to live contentedly.[16] It's our masters' own fault, after all, so let them pay for it.

NURSE: And you can be sure they will, since they're in prison.

GILLET: Let them settle their differences there if they want to! Let them snarl and show their teeth like a couple of dogs fighting over a bone! In the meantime we'll have some fun.

FELIPPES: By God, you're right, Gillet. I never knew a man who saw things more clearly than you.

GILLET: Shall we do it properly, then? Let's go and eat and drink in style at a tavern near here where I was earlier to-day. There we'll amuse ourselves like gentlemen — after all, isn't that what our masters do most of the time?

FELIPPES: A splendid idea! But you haven't laid in a stock of game for us to shoot our blunderbusses at.

GILLET: There's no need: the chambermaid there is the prettiest girl you've ever seen.

FELIPPES: Let's go then. But, alas, what about our masters?

GILLET: What about them?

FELIPPES: All right, let's be off then, let's get out of here.

GILLET: Good-bye, Nurse.

NURSE: That's right, run along! A loyal pair of servants you are! Still, from what I've heard, Restitue is well avenged on Filadelfe. Won't Dame Jacqueline be surprised when she hears about this! And his father Benard de Metz will be even more surprised if he ever comes here. I wonder, too, what Gerard, Euvertre's father, will say. And Fremin, when he finds out that someone has tried to abduct his daughter. As for me, I'm going to hide somewhere and not say a word about all this to anyone.

SCENE VII   ALIZON

ALIZON: Don't worry about a thing, Fleurdelys, and don't cry. And stay indoors while I go where I told you. — May my name never be mentioned again by any living soul if I don't take my revenge on Claude and make him pay for what he's done, and if I don't persuade Fremin to give the scoundrel the punishment he deserves. Then at any rate he'll know for sure whether I'm all he takes me for. I'll see to it that the whole blame is put on his shoulders, since he's already in prison with the others. But didn't Fremin say he would be at Captain Chandiou's house? I must go and speak to him there.

ACT IV

SCENE I   GILLET

GILLET: What bad luck! Our drinking party at the tavern
was cut short by the unexpected arrival of Sieur
Benard, my master's father. I left quickly to come
here and tell Dame Jacqueline. But how can I let my
master know too? Oh Fortune, how wondrous are
your deeds! Why did you decree that this man, who
has come all the way from Metz, should arrive here
on such an unfortunate day? As a result, he'll be
greeted with the most delightful news about his son
— and what's even worse, he's interrupted our feast.
But there he is already, with his servant; it won't
be long now before the shouting starts. Still, why
should I worry about that? Let them argue it out
among themselves. In the meantime I'll go back to
the tavern where I left my pal swilling large quanti-
ties of wine.[17]

SCENE II   BENARD (an old man), FELIX (his lackey)

BENARD: Didn't I tell you we'd never find our way about
this big city, with its maze of streets? How are you
feeling, Felix? Aren't you very tired?

FELIX: Of course I'm tired — what do you expect, after
tramping round this city for so long, and after all the
trouble we had getting here from your home in

33

Lorraine? If we could at least have eaten something
at the inn where we've put up! But you were in such
a hurry to see your son, you didn't give me a chance
to snatch even a bite.

BENARD: It's true, I'm longing to see him. I'm worried that
he may have got into difficulties or have lost weight
since I saw him last. But you must agree that I am
fortunate to be moving to such a fine city and to
have left our wretched province which has been so
constantly troubled by wars.

FELIX: I'm very much afraid we may have left purgatory
for hell.

BENARD: But have you ever seen a city whose inhabitants were so polite and well-mannered?

FELIX: Why couldn't one of them have offered us a drink
then, for heaven's sake?

BENARD: You haven't answered my question. I'm telling
you that this is the most beautiful city in the world,
with the most beautiful streets, the most beautiful
houses, the most beautiful churches, the most beautiful monasteries, and the most beautiful palaces.

FELIX: You may say what you like, but to me there is no
more beautiful sight in this city than the appetizing
cook-shops whose delicious odours I've been smelling
as we've walked past them.

BENARD: You think only of what befits your nature,
animal that you are.

FELIX: Why, you know very well . . .

BENARD: Be quiet! I wonder who the lady is coming out of
that house.

SCENE III   JACQUELINE, BENARD, FELIX

JACQUELINE: Dear God, how my daughter has deceived me!

BENARD: I believe this is the house where my son is staying.

JACQUELINE: Where, wretched woman that I am, where can I find the vile degenerate who has dishonoured my daughter?

FELIX: I wonder who she's getting so steamed up about.

JACQUELINE: As God is my witness, I'll scratch his eyes out with my nails and tear him into pieces, if only I could lay hands on him.

BENARD: I believe I know that lady.

FELIX: Didn't I say, Sir, that we'd arrived in hell? There's Proserpina herself.[18]

JACQUELINE: If only his father were here in this city now! I'd tell him very frankly what I thought of him for sending me such a virtuous young man.

BENARD: Heaven help me! Unless my eyes deceive me, that is Dame Jacqueline to whom I sent my son. I must speak to her. —God save you, Dame Jacqueline, I'm very glad to see you. How are you? And how is my son Filadelfe? Don't you recognize me? I am . . .

JACQUELINE: Ha, God keep you, Seigneur Benard! You've certainly come at the right moment. There's nothing I wanted more than a chance to give you a piece of my mind. A curse on you, fair sir, for sending such a wicked son to my house! May the devil break his bones and legs, and yours too!

FELIX: What a charming greeting!

BENARD: Keep quiet! I'm afraid this woman has lost her reason since I last saw her.

JACQUELINE: I wish your son had broken his neck the day he first set foot in my house.

BENARD: But what harm has my son done you?

JACQUELINE: What harm, dear God? I'd like to see him swing from the gallows, and you too for sending him to me.

FELIX: Madam, I beg you, let's not start a quarrel, for we haven't had any supper yet. I don't know what's on your mind, but I beseech you, let's talk instead about going into your house, for we're very tired and thirsty.

BENARD: Will you be quiet, you donkey!

JACQUELINE: Knave! Scoundrel! Did you send your son to me so that he should ruin me? You're a wicked and depraved man. It wouldn't take me much to . . .

FELIX: What delightful Parisian courtesy! From what I can see, we're doomed to starve. Didn't you say, Sir, that the people in this city were so polite?

BENARD: Away with you, rascal, since you can't keep quiet!

FELIX: Yes, I'd much rather go and find a place to eat.

BENARD: Go to the devil!

FELIX: I'd sooner go the little devil in this city and reclaim the interest on the time I've lost in not drinking. I'm leaving the two of you to quarrel to your hearts' content.

BENARD: Now tell me, Dame Jacqueline, what leads you to insult me so, on account of my son? What do you reproach him with? What do you hold against me? Such insults are unseemly in a lady like yourself, and doubly so when they are addressed to me.

JACQUELINE: Have I perhaps not cause for complaint, you unspeakable villain?

BENARD: Why don't you tell me what this is all about?

JACQUELINE: Your son has brought dishonour on my family, in return for the kindness I have shown him.

BENARD: But what has he done?

JACQUELINE: He's raped my daughter, if you must know.

BENARD: Raped? But that's impossible! He's only a young lad.

JACQUELINE: Only a young lad, is he? Your young lad, it grieves me to say, has given my daughter another little lad.

BENARD (aside): Alas, must the father now bear the blame for his son's misdeeds? I arrived in this city full of joy, looking forward to spending my remaining days in peace here with my son and this lady, and instead I find myself caught up in an even fiercer war than the one I got away from.

JACQUELINE: You must admit that I have greater cause for concern than you. Where shall I ever find a man now who'll want to take my daughter for his wife? She won't dare show her face before her friends again, she won't dare go to any more social meetings or public gatherings. Her plight is already known all over the town. Soon people will be making up tales and songs about her in the city squares. And women lying in childbirth will be talking about nothing else but what's happened to my daughter and me. Everyone will point the finger of scorn at us.

BENARD: But where is that wicked young man? If only I could see him and talk to him, I'd soon let him know how angry I am.

JACQUELINE: He hasn't been in the house all day.

BENARD: Where can I find him then? Alas, what I need is peace, not anxiety. Perhaps those persons over there can tell me where he is.

JACQUELINE: That's possible. One of them is a neighbour of mine who knows him well.

SCENE IV   FREMIN, ALIZON, JACQUELINE, BENARD

FREMIN: But are you really quite certain that Fleurdelys
   is in no way to blame for this affair? Nor you, for
   that matter?

ALIZON: I've told you a hundred times, it's that wretched
   Claude who's responsible for it all; he's the one who
   let them in with all their weapons.

FREMIN: All the same, I can't help feeling that you must
   have had a hand in this business. I ought never to
   have entrusted her to your care.

ALIZON: No, it's your own fault for not finding a husband
   for her before now. I was always afraid something
   like this might happen.

FREMIN: By my soul, I assure you she'll be married to the
   very first man who asks me for her hand. I only
   wish I could find her parents before that.

JACQUELINE: Seigneur Fremin, do you perhaps know
   where Filadelfe is, the young man who lodges in my
   house?

FREMIN: Isn't he one of the two young men you say have
   been taken off to prison, Alizon?

BENARD: My son Filadelfe is in prison?

FREMIN: What? This Filadelfe is your son?

JACQUELINE: Yes.

FREMIN: Well, well, that's a charming son you have, my
   dear sir — such a fine character, such high principles!
   If you knew the foul turn he's done me to-day, you'd
   wish you'd never sired him.

BENARD (*aside*): Dear God, what fresh misfortune is this?
   It's just one calamity after another, and each worse
   than the one before. Everyone is complaining about
   my son. Whom am I to believe? — But tell me, why is
   my son in prison?

FREMIN: My dear sir, you son is where he deserves to be, I assure you. And now I must get back to my house to set my affairs in order and find out the truth of the whole matter from my daughter.

BENARD: Alas, what a terrible situation I'm in!

ALIZON: You've a very wicked son. He and his band of armed ruffians have tried to abduct this gentleman's daughter with whom he fell in love all of two months ago.

BENARD: Good heavens! I'm . . .

JACQUELINE: So it wasn't enough for him to carry on an illicit affair with my daughter, he had to make love to this other girl too, the wretched scoundrel.

ALIZON: He forced his way into our house and seized hold of the girl, but then Filandre, the officer of the watch, arrived and quickly marched them off to prison, him and that other young man who'd come for the same purpose.

BENARD: This business will be the death of me.

JACQUELINE: You can live or die, please yourself. I'm going back into the house to give my daughter another good talking-to and tell her the news.

BENARD: Won't you stay a few moments longer? I'd like to ask you . . .

JACQUELINE: I haven't the time. You can go on chattering to yourself if you want to.

ALIZON: I must be off too. I can hear my master calling me.

BENARD: Dear Lord in heaven above, what am I to do? What can I say? Whom can I turn to? Everyone has forsaken me; I have lost all solace, all hope and happiness. Nothing can compare with this calamity - not even the loss of my daughter and my possessions in Metz during the war, nor the death of my

parents and friends. Vile son, you have destroyed
my life and ruined my reputation. Did I send you to
this city so that you should commit such foul deeds?
Cursed be the day, the hour and the moment when I
begot you! Let this be a warning to all men not
to long so much for children of their own: though
they may show great promise in their youth, it takes
very little nowadays to corrupt them completely. If
only I had my daughter Fleurdelys with me now,
whom I lost so long ago, I wouldn't hesitate to
disown this accursed Filadelfe as my son. But since
he's the only child I have left, I can't very well leave
him to his fate, but shall have to try and obtain his
release. Only I'm so tired, I can barely put one foot
in front of the other. —But there's that man again
whose good graces I must obtain if I want to get that
wretched son of mine set free.

SCENE V   FREMIN, BENARD

FREMIN: Worthy sir, your extreme despair, your bitter
   tears and heart-rending sobs have compelled me
   to come out to speak to you. They would, as the
   saying goes, have moved stones and rocks and even
   the fiercest beasts on earth to pity. I wish to offer
   you comfort, help and counsel, for I am a man and
   therefore one with all mankind.[19]

BENARD: I don't know how to thank you for your kind
   and gracious offer. Your courtesy leads me think
   that you are not a native of this city whose inhabitants are so lacking in politeness.

FREMIN: No, indeed; I was born in Picardy.

BENARD: That explains it. Since you have so generously
   offered me your compassion, I beg you not to demand
   retribution for the wrong you claim my son has done
   to you and to your daughter's honour; please forgive

him his grievous offence. Do not torment my poor, feeble old age with legal investigations and proceedings, with writs and lawsuits. Do not make me fall prey to the greedy and grasping lawyers of this city; they would strip me of everything in less than no time: flesh, bones, possessions.

FREMIN: You are right there.

BENARD: I acknowledge my son's guilt; but won't you forgo at least some of the retribution you are entitled to exact? Just think what follies youth and passionate love can make a man commit. And remember that you alone have the power to secure his release. I am ready to give you whatever satisfaction you may demand.

FREMIN: My dear sir, I have travelled far and wide and have visited many places, including Metz where I know you come from; and my experiences confirm the truth of what you say. I'm well acquainted with the ways of love and youth. Moreover, whether here or in my own province, I would consider myself your friend and would try to accommodate you in this or any other matter.

BENARD: I'm most grateful to you, believe me.

FREMIN: But quite apart from such considerations, I'm especially inclined to grant your request because you are mistaken about Fleurdelys's family and her place of birth.

BENARD: I never want to hear the name 'Fleurdelys' again! But go on.

FREMIN: Why do you say that?

BENARD: It revives old griefs in me, since that was the name of my daughter, the little girl I lost. I don't know to this day whether she's alive or dead.

FREMIN: How very sad! Where did you become separated from her?

BENARD: In the city of Metz.

FREMIN: In Metz! When?

BENARD: When the French entered the city. But why these questions? It only increases my grief to speak about this. Do finish what you were going to say.

FREMIN: No, no, go on. I have my reasons for wanting to know more about this. In what circumstances did you lose her?

BENARD: I left her behind in my house by accident, in my hurry to escape from the city; for the French had pitched camp outside Toul not far from Metz, and several of us citizens were afraid of what might happen with such a large royal army taking up position so close-by — especially since we had sided with the Emperor rather than with the King and might therefore have been regarded as traitors to the French cause. Of course, if I'd known that our city would surrender as it did, I would never have left. Anyway, when the Constable of France marched into the city with a large band of his soldiers, some of them entered my house. But what's the point of my telling you all this?

FREMIN: Dear God, I believe I was right in what I suspected from the outset! You say you left your daughter alone in the house? How old would she have been?

BENARD: Five years.

FREMIN: That fits in perfectly. And she was called Fleurdelys?

BENARD: Yes, she was. But what is the use of all these questions?

FREMIN: Be patient a little while longer. If you should happen to meet her, would you recognize her?

BENARD: I hardly think so. But wait: if I remember rightly, she had a small red mark like a strawberry under her left ear, caused by a fall. But why are you questioning me so carefully? Dear God, is it possible that you can give me some news of her?

FREMIN: Is there any chance that God will grant me to-day what I have so fervently wished for many times? Shall I be freed from worry and anxiety at last? Listen now to what I started to tell you a moment ago, and then judge for yourself whether I'm really speaking about your daughter. As I told you, I feel especially inclined to grant your request concerning your son because you are mistaken about the family and place of origin of Fleurdelys, the girl your son tried to abduct.

BENARD: What! Isn't she your daughter?

FREMIN: No, although most people in this city think so. But I've never had any children and, in any case, the girl comes from Metz.

BENARD: Then tell me, please, how she fell into your hands.

FREMIN: To tell you the truth, I've never discovered who her real father was. You should know that I was a soldier for some twenty years. For most of that time I served under the command of the Constable you've just mentioned, and so I was among those who entered Metz with him. Once inside the city, I went in search of billets, like many of my comrades, and I entered a house where I found much private property but not a living soul except a little girl about four or five years old.

BENARD: Oh Fortune, is it possible that you are really granting me the happiness of seeing my daughter again?

FREMIN: As soon as the little girl caught sight of me, she called me 'Father'. This touched me so profoundly that I kept her by me and later sent her to my house in

Picardy, where my wife, who had borne me no children herself, brought her up as our own daughter.

BENARD: What clothes was she wearing when you found her?

FREMIN: A short dress of shot-silk; and she had a pearl hanging from her ear. She often called out the name 'Laurence'.

BENARD: That was her nurse's name. There's no doubt about it: she really is my daughter. I beg you to let me see her soon — as soon as possible. It couldn't be soon enough for me.

FREMIN: With all my heart. Let's go inside.

BENARD: I wonder if she looks like her poor departed mother.

FREMIN: Believe me, sir, you'll find that she is a very beautiful girl, with a lovely figure.

ACT V

SCENE I GERARD (father of Euvertre)

GERARD: Can my son really have been so wicked, so depraved, so brazen, as to force his way armed into a house, with the intention of defiling the honour of the owner's daughter? Did he really commit such a mad and outrageous deed during the short time that I was away from home? Didn't he feel any shame? Didn't he fear his father's anger? I'm so incensed and furious that I shall die if I cannot soon vent my rage on him. If only I had allowed him to marry this girl when he was so constantly pestering me for my permission. I believe it was my harsh refusal which drove him to commit this act of folly. — Ah, there's the man I've come to see about getting my son released from the prison where I'm told he's being held.

SCENE II FREMIN, BENARD, GERARD

FREMIN: Though I am almost heart-broken at the thought of losing my adopted daughter whom I love so dearly, I am happy that she's found her father again. Well, didn't I tell you that she was virtuous, modest and beautiful?

BENARD: You did indeed. I shall be forever grateful to you for giving her such a fine upbringing and training. Did you notice how bashful and embarrassed she was when I raised her hair a little above her left ear, to see if I could identify her by the red mark I'd described to you?

GERARD (*aside*): I'd better not interrupt their conversation just yet.

FREMIN: Yes, I did — but how she wept from sheer happiness when she recognized you! And with what heart-felt pleasure she received her father's embraces.

BENARD: But what do you think of my son being so wicked as to feel illicit love for his own sister and plotting such an outrage against her?

FREMIN: He didn't know then who her real parents were. But I've just had an idea — tell me what you think of it. Why not make him marry this Restitue you spoke to me about? and give Fleurdelys in marriage to Euvertre who has so often asked me for her hand.

GERARD (*aside*): Didn't he just mention my son?

FREMIN: Wouldn't that be a good solution?

BENARD: An excellent one! Didn't I tell you that I would agree to whatever you proposed?

GERARD: May God protect you, Seigneur Fremin! I've been told that my son . . .

FREMIN: This, my dear sir, is the father of Euvertre, the young man we were just talking about.

GERARD: . . . has created some disturbance outside your house.

FREMIN: Sieur Gerard, it's not with me that you should speak about this matter but with this gentleman here. He is the father of the girl your son is so much in love with.

GERARD: But aren't you her father?

FREMIN: No, I was only her adoptive father. This is her real father who has only recently arrived in this city. We'll explain to you later how he recognized her.

GERARD: May I ask you, sir . . .

BENARD: My dear sir, I know very well what you wish to say to me, and I should be very ungracious if I didn't show you the same kindness and courtesy as this good gentleman has extended to me, for he most generously granted me a similar request I made when I still thought that my daughter was his child.

FREMIN: But do you know what we were proposing a moment ago?

GERARD: What?

FREMIN: You were reluctant before to allow your son to marry this gentleman's new-found daughter, because I couldn't offer a large enough dowry. Will you withdraw your objection, now that the girl has another and far wealthier father who is one of the leading citizens of Metz?

GERARD: I must admit that you scratch me where I itch! Yes, I shall be delighted with such a match if he is satisfied with it.

BENARD: Very satisfied indeed.

FREMIN: In that case, all that remains for us is to appease Dame Jacqueline. Let's inform her of our proposals, and then she'll have no further cause to feel angry with us.

GERARD: There's Filandre, the officer of the watch; he comes at the right moment. I'm sure that when he knows about our arrangements, he'll be quite willing to release his prisoners.

FREMIN: As you know, he is in our debt because of some favours we've done him in the past.

SCENE III   FILANDRE (officer of the watch),
                    FREMIN, BENARD, GERARD

FILANDRE: I wonder what Sieur Gerard, Seigneur Fremin
    and Dame Jacqueline think of me for keeping these
    two young men and the servant under arrest in my
    house.[20] I'm on very good terms with them and
    should therefore like to settle this matter to their
    satisfaction before it goes any further.

FREMIN: Sir, we'd like to ask you . . .

FILANDRE: But there they are, just the people I was
    looking for! — Well, what can you find to say in
    defence of these three men?

FREMIN: We were just going to invite you to come into
    Dame Jacqueline's house where you'll hear a truly
    amazing tale. We'll talk about the prisoners after-
    wards.

FILANDRE: Very well, let's go in. But you'll appreciate
    that I can't reasonably detain them in my house for
    very long before I'll have to hand them over to the
    courts.

BENARD: Let's all go in then. But I wonder where that
    rascally servant of mine has got to.

SCENE IV   GILLET, FELIX, FELIPPES (servants)

GILLET: A plague on all skinflints who hoard their money!
    But what did you think of that beauty?

FELIX: I'd call her a real gem! One often has to work on
    far worse stones.

GILLET: Haven't we lived it up like true gentlemen?

FELIX: As for me, I'd gladly give up Paradise itself if I
    could always lead such a life on earth. Fortune be
    praised for making me go, without my knowing
    why, to the tavern where you both were.

GILLET: God knew how badly you needed buddies like us and sent you there Himself. We were already hard at it when you arrived, but you certainly made us set to again with a new will. Why are you so quiet, Felippot? What's making you so melancholy?

FELIPPES: I'm afraid the wine I drank has gone to my head. It's beginning to affect me.

GILLET: Let's go and find our old master, Felix, and tell him he's arrived just in time to pay our bill for us.

FELIPPES: And what's to become of me? Now that I think of it, I wonder what's happened to my young master. Where is he? Good Lord, I'd quite forgotten that he's in prison — I really must be drunk. It's high time I thought of him. But who are those people coming out of Dame Jacqueline's house? Good heavens, isn't that my old master? What the devil is he doing talking to the officer of the watch? Perhaps he's asking him to arrest me! I'd better push off.

SCENE V   FILANDRE, FREMIN, BENARD, GERARD,
                     JACQUELINE

FILANDRE: Since God, in His mysterious and providential ways, has brought these things to pass, who am I to prevent them from coming to a successful and happy conclusion?

FREMIN: Sir, since you are willing to hand them over to us without further ado, what do you think of playing a little practical joke on them?

FILANDRE: How shall we do that?

FREMIN: Bring them here bound and in chains, without telling them anything — just to give them a good fright so that we can see the looks on their faces.

FILANDRE: An excellent idea! I can have them here very soon, for they're not far away.

GERARD: Go and get them then. You have to admit this Filandre is an honest and upright man — the only officer of the law who is. The rest of them are a greedy lot, and intent only on their personal gain. They amass the proceeds of a million trivial lawsuits, while making a pretence of keeping the peace.

FREMIN: How well everything has turned out for us!

BENARD: I'm delighted we've made such satisfactory arrangements.

JACQUELINE: My only regret is that I insulted you and offered you such a rude welcome.

BENARD: Dame Jacqueline, don't give it another thought! Anyone moved by righteous anger would have done the same.

FREMIN: You know, I've just thought what you ought to do.

BENARD: Please tell us.

FREMIN: As you know, Dame Jacqueline is a most virtuous, honest and wealthy lady.

BENARD: I'm certain of it.

FREMIN: She is unattached, independent, and beholden to no-one. She runs an excellent household, has an attractive home, and is well provided with all the necessities of life. She's not involved in any disputes with sons-in-law or daughters-in-law, sisters or cousins, or relatives of her late husband.

BENARD: What are you getting at?

FREMIN: I'm thinking that the two of you would make a very good match.

BENARD: What!

FREMIN: Since the son is marrying the daughter, why shouldn't the father marry the mother?

BENARD: What, me marry her?

FREMIN: Yes, why not?

GERARD: You know, Fremin's suggestion is an excellent one.

BENARD: But what do the rest of you say to that? Would you advise me, a man approaching sixty, to marry a lady who's not much younger than myself?

GERARD: I certainly would. You'll find it an excellent arrangement, especially since you haven't yet established a household of your own in this city.

BENARD: What do you say, Dame Jacqueline?

JACQUELINE: And you yourself?

BENARD: I shall abide by your decision.

JACQUELINE: And I by yours.

BENARD: In that case, I accept with pleasure.

JACQUELINE: And so do I.

FREMIN: God be praised for everything! Now we'll have three weddings instead of two.

GERARD: Look, aren't those our prisoners approaching?

BENARD: Yes. Let's put on suitable expressions.

SCENE VI   FILADELFE, EUVERTRE, CLAUDE
(a servant), FILANDRE, FREMIN, GERARD,
BENARD

FILADELFE: Good heavens, are they going to put us to death already?

EUVERTRE: Where are they taking us? I wish to God I'd never been born.

CLAUDE: My life isn't worth ten cents now, poor wretch that I am!

FILANDRE: Don't cry before you've been flogged! We have some very different games and entertainments in store for you.

FILADELFE: I wish I were dead already. Whatever would
    my father say if he heard of this! If only he wasn't so
    far away.

FILANDRE: Now attend to your case! Here are those who
    will judge you and pronounce the final sentence.

EUVERTRE: What! Have we already been tried?

FILANDRE: If you are wise, you won't appeal their
    sentence.

CLAUDE: I can already feel the hangman's rope.

FILANDRE: Honourable judges, I herewith deliver these
    prisoners into your hands, so that you may decide
    what should be done with them. You there, kneel
    down and don't lower your eyes like that!

EUVERTRE: Good God, isn't that my father over there? Oh
    earth, open up and swallow me!

CLAUDE: Good heavens, there's my master! I'm done for.

FREMIN: Why are you staring so hard at this gentleman,
    Filadelfe? One might think you'd seen him before.

FILADELFE: Dear God, surely that's my father! He must
    have come here from Metz. Good Lord, I wish I were
    a hundred feet underground.

FREMIN (aside): He's filled with shame and remorse for
    his crime. That's to his credit.

BENARD (aside): I can't contain myself any longer —
    I must embrace him. —Oh my son, my dear son!

FREMIN: How touching a father's love is!

FILADELFE: Father, I beg you, forgive me the wicked deed
    I've committed and do not punish me as I deserve. I
    admit that I've sinned grievously.

EUVERTRE: Father, forgive me too, I beseech you.

BENARD: But, Filadelfe, you've only mentioned the of-
    fence you committed to-day. What about the wrong
    you did to Dame Jacqueline's daughter?

FILADELFE: My God, do you know about that too? In that case I agree that I deserve to be punished, and I no longer ask you to forgive me.

FREMIN: Nevertheless the three of you will not be punished as you deserve. But, firstly, to explain the situation to you . . .

FILANDRE: Now for the sentences!

FREMIN: ... I must tell you, Filadelfe, that the girl you tried to abduct by force is your own sister.

FILADELFE: What! Fleurdelys is my sister?

FREMIN: Yes. We'll tell you later how she came to be recognized.

GERARD: Secondly, as for you, Euvertre, it has been decided that you shall marry this sister of Filadelfe's, whom you planned to ravish. Therefore put an end to your quarrel, both of you, and live like brothers from now on.

EUVERTRE: With all my heart!

BENARD: Thirdly, you, Filadelfe, shall marry Restitue who, as you can see, is quite well again. After all, she's the one you loved so much at the beginning. And at the same time, I shall marry her mother.

FILADELFE: That makes me very happy.

FILANDRE: This shall be your punishment, then. You men there, remove their chains!

FILADELFE: Is it possible that what I hear and see is really happening? Or am I dreaming?

EUVERTRE: I can barely credit what I see with my own eyes. Such joy, contentment and happiness — are they really to be mine?

CLAUDE: As for me, I don't think I'm dreaming, for I can see and feel the chains coming off.

GERARD: Now that I see my son free again, I'm the happiest and most contented man in the whole world.

BENARD: I thought I would find myself without a friend or acquaintance in this city. But now, praise be to God, just counting those present here, I have as many as if I had always lived here.

FREMIN: And I who also came from another city, am I not fortunate to have the support and friendship of all of you here!

FILADELFE: But how did all this come about?

FREMIN: Let's go inside — we have much to tell you.

FILADELFE: Before we go in, Father, I'd like to ask you, if you love me, to be generous towards Claude, Fremin's servant, who has rendered me many useful services.

BENARD: He won't be forgotten, I assure you. And you, Seigneur Filandre, and all the rest of you, don't fail to honour us with your presence at the three wedding celebrations.

FILANDRE: We'll be more than pleased to come.

FILANDELFE (*to the audience*): Fare well, gentlemen. And if our play has found favour with you, please show it by your applause.

Notes to the play

1. For the sake of uniformity, the forms 'Filadelfe', 'Filandre', and 'Felippes' are used throughout this translation, although the original text offers also the variants 'Philadelfe', 'Philandre', and 'Felippe'. No acute accents have been added to any of the names.

2. See Introduction, section on 'Historical background'.

3. The remark evidently carries strong sexual overtones.

4. Another image with overt sexual connotations, and which is at the same time typical of the Nurse's robust humor and her unpuritanical moral outlook.

5. It is not at all clear from Restitue's remark, or from those made by the Nurse, what they propose to do about the baby. The French text — 'que je soys bien tost delivree de cest enfant— ' is doubly ambiguous. Firstly, because 'délivrer une femme . . .' can mean either 'to deliver a woman of a child' (i.e. a reference to the child's birth) or 'to deliver a woman from, to rid her of, the child' (i.e. after its birth). And secondly, if one opts for the latter meaning, as the critics have done, there is the uncertainty as to what kind of 'deliverance' is envisaged. The same expression is used at the end of this scene by the Nurse when she assures Restitue that they will find a thousand ways 'pour vous delivrer de vostre enfant'. The Nurse's further remark that she knows 'un tour de maitrise' ('a marvellous trick' or perhaps, in a wider sense, 'a marvellous solution') led

P. Toldo to speculate that she might be contemplating an abortion or infanticide ('La Comédie francaise . . .', V (1898), 561, n.1). In their edition of *Les Corrivaus* (p. 205, n.3), K.M. Hall and C.N. Smith point out that both actions were considered capital offences at the time, and they suggest that what is being planned is the abandoning of the child to a foster-mother. In any case, the Nurse's earlier statement to Restitue that she is confident of finding a way 'to save both your honour and your child' surely rules out the interpretation proposed by Toldo.

6. An obvious clue to the denouement! For another, see Felippes's remark about Filadelfe in II.i.

7. Many scenes begin or end with a soliloquy which does not form a separate scene (a striking example is II.i which opens with Euvertre's monologue and closes with that of Felippes). Usually in those cases the moment when a new character enters or when a character already onstage exits can be clearly deduced from the text (but see n.11 on the end of I.iv where there is a slight risk of ambiguity).

8. The salamander was popularly believed to be able to live in fire which, however, it quenched by the chill of its body. François I adopted as his badge a salamander in the midst of flames, with the legend *Nutrisco et extinguo* ('I nourish and extinguish').

9. The gist of Gillet's argument is as follows: Just as alchemists seek to transmute baser metals into gold, so those Christians who practise sexual continence during Lent are intent on extracting a purer, spiritual essence from sensual passion. In so doing, they exchange the substance of love for its shadow.

10. The French text 'à fin qu'en cest affaire icy, tu me serves d'un O en chiffre' has puzzled La Taille's editors. K.M. Hall and C.N. Smith interpret it as meaning that 'Gillet counts for nothing ('O'), but 0 allied with 1=10', which is ingenious but not wholly convincing. D.L. Drysdall wonders whether one should not insert 'ne' between 'tu' and 'me' - with 'O' again signifying 'uselessness'. It might be added that the word 'chiffre' itself evoked the idea of a person of no importance or authority.

11. Gillet's final remark ('for . . . us') is pronounced after Filadelfe has left the stage.

12. These ironic questions are intended to stress Alizon's low morals (cf. n.13 and Felippe's comment in II.i). Bawds in learned comedy often make a pretence of great piety (e.g. Françoise in Odet de Turnèbe's *Les Contents* — see D.A. Beecher's translation in this series). Low Sunday (or Quasimodo Sunday) is the Sunday after Easter, and thus the last day of the octave of Easter. The reference to the wounds of St. Francis of Assisi recalls his stigmatization on Mount Alvernia in 1224. At the same time, the French words *quasimodo* and *plaie* could denote a woman's pudenda in vulgar speech.

13. No doubt an allusion to Alizon's past activities as a bawd.

14. A diminutive of 'Felippes', denoting affection.

15. It will be noted that Gillet's account differs from that given by Felippes (III.v), according to which Euvertre rushed into the house on hearing Fleurdelys's and Alizon's screams. This could be regarded as an understandable assumption on the part of Felippes who was unaware of the arrangements made by Euvertre and Alizon. It may, however, be deduced from Gillet's account that Alizon, alarmed by the attack on Fleurdelys, hurriedly signalled to Euvertre to enter the house.

16. Nostradamus (1503-1566), the French astrologer, became famous through his prophecies, first published at Lyons in 1555 (an expanded edition appeared there in 1568). The reflection here attributed to him by Gillet has not been identified by La Taille's editors. Drysdall thinks that it may have been made up by La Taille himself.

17. 'swilling . . . of wine': the precise meaning of the French 'laissant passer les plus chargez' is not clear.

18. Proserpina was the wife of Pluto and therefore Queen of the lower world.

19. After Terence, *Heauton timorumenos*, 77: 'Homo sum; humani nil me alienum puto' ('I am a man, I consider nothing human alien to me').

20. La Taille writes: 'que je tienne dans mon logis de *leurs gents* (lit.: 'some of their people') comme en prison'; but, in fact, no relative or servant of Jacqueline's is involved.